King of England James I

The essayes of a prentise, in the divine art of poesie

A counterblast to tobacco. London, 1604

King of England James I

The essayes of a prentise, in the divine art of poesie
A counterblast to tobacco. London, 1604

ISBN/EAN: 9783337108298

Printed in Europe, USA, Canada, Australia, Japan

Cover: Foto ©Andreas Hilbeck / pixelio.de

More available books at **www.hansebooks.com**

English Reprints.

JAMES VI of Scotland, I of England.

The Essayes of a Prentise, in the Divine Art of Poesie.

Edinburgh. 1585.

A Counterblaste to Tobacco.

London. 1604.

CAREFULLY EDITED BY

EDWARD ARBER.

Associate, King's College, London, F.R.G.S., &c.

LONDON:

5 QUEEN SQUARE, BLOOMSBURY.

Ent. Stat. Hall.]   10 December, 1869.   [*All Rights reserved.*

CONTENTS.

INTRODUCTION.

Iterature is a Republic that admits of no authority but that of Learning, Genius, and Perſuaſion. The Writer—whether King, Peer, or Commoner—is judged with one judgment. Curioſity, Reverence, or Loyalty may procure for a Work an attentive reception and ſome preſent applauſe : but its perpetuation, its place in the Literature of the country, will depend upon either its intrinſic merits, or on its illuſtrative power in reſpeČt to the age in which it was written.

On theſe latter grounds, the Royal produČtions here reprinted have been admitted into the Series.

The Reulis and Cautelis in Scottis Poeſie bring James VI. within the ſucceſſion of our early Poetical Critics; whoſe writings—not very numerous, but now exceſſively ſcarce—are of great value in the ſtudy of Engliſh Poetry. For—not to ſpeak of their often preſerving ſnatches of poems now utterly loſt—they ſhow us the theories of verſification, the canons of Poetic taſte and ſtyle, prevailing in our country, immediately before the advent of Spenſer, Shakeſpeare, and their fertile contemporaries. Theſe writings were reprinted by Mr. Haſlewood in his *Ancient Critical Eſſays*, 2 vols. 4to,, 1811-16 : a Reprint, of which only 300 copies were printed, (and a portion of that number deſtroyed by fire), which is now ſcarce ; and which, when met with, uſually coſts two or three pounds. The original texts being ſo rare ; Mr. Haſlewood's Reprint was, until lately, the only means whereby moſt of us could obtain a knowledge of this important department of our National literature.

In purſuance, therefore, of what ſeemed an imperative duty : theſe Criticiſms in Poeſy are being gradually reproduced in this Series. To the four now publiſhed—GASCOIGNE, SIDNEY, JAMES VI., and PUTTENHAM : we purpoſe adding in 1870, W. WEBBE's *Diſcourſe* (of which only two copies remain): and the five produČtions, forming two-thirds of Mr. Haſlewood's Reprint — including alſo with them four others of a differing character—will be obtainable for 5s. 6d., and be on *unlimited* fale. It is to be hoped that this advantageous facility of knowledge, may allure many to a more thorough delight in Elizabethan poetry: and that by a combined study of these Principles of Poesy with the Poems themselves, many may attain to a more subtle appreciation, a more sensitive feeling of that Song—which, in its aggregate and bulk, is the sweetest and most enchanting in our History.

How much the *Counterblaste* represents another class of our Literature, and a good deal of our former manners: the notices given of the Tobacco controversy will show. Thus both works stand on their own merits; their own reputation and that of their Royal Author but predisposing them to a courteous reception.

What he says in the Preface to his other poetical work, *Exercises at vacant houres*, must not be forgotten in considering the *Essayes,* or Attempts of an Apprentise :

And in case thou finde aswel in this work, as in my LEPANTO following, many incorrect errours, both in the dytement and orthography, I must pray thee to accept this my reasonable excuse, which is this. Thou considers, I doubt not, that vpon the one part, I composed these things in my verie young and tender yeares : wherein nature, except shee were a monster can admit of no perfection. And nowe on the other parte, being of riper yeares, my burden is so great and continuall, without anie intermission, that when my ingyne and age could, my affaires and fasherie wo-ld not permit mee, to remark the wr—ng orthography committed by the copiars of my vnlegible and ragged hand, far les to amend my proper errours : Yea scarslie but at stollen moments, haue I the leasure to blenk vpon any paper, and yet not that, with free and vnvexed spirit. Alwaies, rough and vnpolished as they are, I offer them vnto thee. . . .

Nothing need here be said of the king's Sonnets and Poems : they appraise themselves. Of the rest, the following may be noted :—

1. Mr. GILLIES, writing, in 1812, his *Pref. Mem.,* see No. 2 on p. 6, states—"Of the recommendatory versifiers T[h]omas H[udson] was the author of a translation of Du Bartas's *History of Judith*, printed at Edinburgh by Thomas Vautrollier, and republished in the works of Du Bartas by Joshua Sylvester." R. H[udson], proba-ly a brother of the preced—g, was also a writer of verses. See an address to him, by Montgomery, in the second volume of Sibbald's *Chronicle.* M. W. F. is obviously Master William Fouler, author of *The Triumphs of Petrarke* and *The Tarant-la of Love,* extant in MS. in the College Library of Edinburgh, of which specimens have been published by Dr. Leyden.

2. GILLAUME DE SALLUSTE, Seigneur DU BARTAS b. 1544—d. 1590 exercised a considerable influence over some of the minor English poets of b s time. Something like mutual laudation passed between the young Scotch king and the French poet. What James says of Du Bartas may be seen at *pp. 20-21.* Not long after these *Essayes,* the king wrote a poem on the battle of Lepanto : in a French translation of which, by Du Bartas, *La Lepanthe,* is the following *Preface from the Translator to the Author,* in which the Frenchman repays the Scot in full :—

IAQUES, *si tu marchois d'un pied mortee ça bas,*
Hardy l'entreprendroy de t'alloner ses pas :
I'estendroy tous mes nerfs, et ma course sacrée
Loing, loing lairroit à dos les aigles de Borée.
Mais puis qu aigle nouueau tu te guindes és cieux,
Collé bas, ie te suy seulement de mes yeux :
Mais plustost du desir : on, si ie me remuë
Ombre ie vole en terre, et toy dedans la nuë.
  He ! fusse ie vrayment, ô Phœnix Escossois,
Ou l'ombre de ton corps, on l'Echo de ta voix.
Si ie n'auoy l'azur, l'or, et l'argent encore
Dont ton plumage astré brillantement s'honnore,
Au moins i'anrey ta forme : et si mon rude vers
N'exprimoit la douceur de tant d'accords diuers,
Il retiendroit quelque air de tes voix plus qu' humaines,
Mais, Pies, taisez vous pous ouyr les Camœnes.

  3. EMANUEL TREMILLIUS, was a Jew, born at Ferrara about 1510. He
became first a Catholic, then a Protestant ; was a celebrated Hebrew scholar,
and died at Sedan on 9th October 1580. His Latin version of the Scriptures
—originally brought out at Frankfort—was first printed in London in 1580,
and again in 1581. 'Out of Tremillius' therefore simply means :—translated
from out of the Latin version of the Psalms, edited by Tremillius.

In the nineteen years intervening between the publication of the works here prefented to the reader,
James publifhed many works at Edinburgh. As among
others, his *Majestys Poetical Exercifes at Vacant houres*,
in 1591, confifting of his tranflation *The Furies* of Du
Bartas, of his own *Lepanto*, and of Du Bartas' render-
ing, *La Lepanthe.* His *Dæmonologie* in 1599. The
anonymous and fecret firft edition—limited to feven
copies—of *Bafilikon Doron* in 1599. When he came
to the Englifh crown, moft of the profe works were
reprinted in London.

  Almoft his firft new literary produc̄tion as King of
Great Britain and Ireland was *A Counterblaste to Tobacco.* So far as limited time and fpace have permitted,
we have, further on, furrounded it with fomewhat of the
antecedent and fubfequent literature of the fubjec̄t.
Lovers of the Pipe fometimes endeavour to stultify
James' Invéctive : by fketching, on an enlarged fcale,
the perfonal habits, the notions and conceits of the fo-
called Britifh Solomon. Here again the Invéctive muft
ftand on its own merits. What it is in itfelf, we can
eftimate. The meafure of its influence—efpecially
when its Royal authorfhip became generally known—
may not now be attainable. As a matter of hiftory ;
it failed in its purpofe. Tobacco fmoking ftill reigneth,
and will yet reign.

𝕿𝖍𝖊 𝕰𝖘𝖘𝖆𝖞𝖊𝖘 𝖔𝖋 𝖆 𝕻𝖗𝖊𝖓𝖙𝖎𝖘𝖊 𝖎𝖓 𝖙𝖍𝖊 𝕯𝖎𝖛𝖎𝖓𝖊 𝕬𝖗𝖙 𝖔𝖋 𝕻𝖔𝖊𝖘𝖎𝖊.

(a) Issues in the Author's lifetime.

I. *As a separate publication.*

1. 1585. Edinburgh. *Editio princeps*: see title on opposite page.
    1 vol. 4to.

II. *With other works.*

None.

b) Issues since the Author's death.

I. *As a separate publication.*

2. 1814. Edinburgh. *The Essayes of a Prentise, in the Divine Art of*
    1 vol. 8vo.   *Poesie*; with a prefatory Memoir by R. P. GILLIES, F.S.A.E.

II. *With other works.*

3. 10 Dec. 1869. Lond. 1 vol. 8vo. *English Reprints*; see title at *p.* 1.

𝕬 𝕮𝖔𝖚𝖓𝖙𝖊𝖗𝖇𝖑𝖆𝖘𝖙𝖊 𝖙𝖔 𝕿𝖔𝖇𝖆𝖈𝖈𝖔.

(a) Issues in the Author's lifetime.

I. *As a separate publication.*

1. 1604. London. *Editio princeps*: see title at *p.* 95. Anonymously pub-
    1 vol. 4to.   lished, and now very scarce. The present edition is re-
    printed from a copy in the Bodleian Library, at Oxford.

II. *With other works.*

2. 1616. London. The [Prose] Workes of James I.. Collected and edited
    1 vol. fol.   by JAMES MONTAGU, Bp. of WINCHESTER. The *Counter-*
    blaste is at *pp.* 211-212.

3. 1619. London. The same translated into Latin, by the same Bishop.
    1 vol. fol.   The *Counterblaste* is translated at *pp.* 189-207. On *p.* 189, it
    has the title of *Misocapnus siue De Abusu Tobacci Lusus*
    Regius: which is thus varied in repetition on *p.* 200, *Miso-*
    capnus, seu lusus Regius de abusu Tobacci.

(b) Issues since the Author's death.

I. *As a separate publication.*

None.

II. *With other works.*

4. 1672. London. Two Broad-Sides against Tobacco: The First given by
    1 vol. 4to.   King JAMES of famous memory, His *Counterblaste to To-*
    bacco. The Second transcribed out of that learned Physician
    Dr. EVERARD MAYNWARINGE, His *Treatise of the Scurvy.*
    . . . . Concluding with Two *Poems* against *Tobacco*
    [*i.e.* an extract of Sylvester's *Tobacco battered*; see *p.* 116]
    and *Coffee.* Collected and published, as very proper for
    this Age, by J. H. . . . . Licensed according to Order.
    June 6, 1672.
    Or with a slightly different title-page, beginning thus—
    King James His *Counterblaste to Tobacco.* To which
    is added a Learned Discourse written by Dr. EVERARD
    MAYNWARINGE, Proving that Tobacco is a procuring Cause
    of the Scurvy. . . . .

5. 1689.   Another Latin Edition of James' prose works. in which
    1 vol. fol.   *Misocapnus* is included.

6. 10 Dec. 1869. London. 1 vol. 8vo. *English Reprints:* see title at *p.* 1.

THE ESSAYES OF

A PRENTISE, IN THE

DIVINE ART OF

POESIE.

Imprinted at Edinburgh, by Thomas
Vautroullier.
1585.

CVM PRIVILEGIO
REGALI.

THE CATALOGVE OF THE
workis heirin conteined.

SONNET.

IF *Martiall* deeds, and practife of the pen
    Haue wonne to auncient *Grece* a worthie fame :
    If Battels bold, and Bookes of learned men
Haue magnified the mightie *Romain* name :
Then place this Prince, who well deferues the fame :
Since he is one of *Mars* and *Pallas* race :
For both the *Godds* in him haue fett in frame
Their vertewes both, which both, he doth embrace.
O Macedon, adornde with heauenly grace,
O Romain ftout, decorde with learned fkill,
The *Monarks* all to thee fhall quite their place :
Thy endles fame fhall all the world fulfill.
    And after thee, none worthier fhalbe feene,
    To fway the *Svvord,* and gaine the *Laurell* greene.

              T. H.

SONNET.

THE glorious *Grekis* in ftately ftyle do blaife [olde:
    The lawde, the conqurour gaue their *Homer*
    The verfes *Cæfar* fong in *Maroes* praife,
The *Romanis* in remembrance depe haue rolde.
Ye *Thefpian Nymphes,* that fuppe the *Nectar* colde,
That from *Parnaffis* forked topp doth fall,
What *Alexander* or *Auguftus* bolde,
May found his fame, whofe vertewes pafs them all ?
O Phæbus, for thy help, heir might I call,
And on *Minerue,* and *Maias* learned fonne :
But fince I know, none was, none is, nor fhall,
Can rightly ring the fame that he hath wonne,
    Then ftay your trauels, lay your pennis adowne,
    For *Cæfars* works, fhall iuftly *Cæfar* crowne.

             R. H.

SONNET.

THe mightie Father of the *Mufes* nyne
    Who mounted thame vpon *Parnafsus* hill,
    Where *Phœbus* faire amidd thefe *Sifters* fyne
With learned toung fatt teaching euer ftill,
Of late yon God declared his woundrous will,
That *Vranie* fhould teach this Prince moft rare :
Syne fhe informed her fcholler with fuch fkill,
None could with him in Poefie compaire.
Lo, heir the fructis, *Nymphe*, of thy fofter faire,
Lo heir (ô noble *Ioue*) thy will is done,
Her charge compleit, as deid doth now declaire.
This work will witneffe, fhe obeyed the fone.
    O *Phœbus* then reioyce with glauncing glore,
    Since that a King doth all thy court decore.

M. VV.

SONNET.

WHen as my minde exemed was from caire,
    Among the *Nymphis* my felf I did repofe :
    Where I gaue eare to one, who did prepaire
Her fugred voice this fequell to difclofe.
Conveine your felfs (ô fifters) doe not lofe
This paffing tyme which hafteth faft away :
And yow who wrytes in ftately verfe and profe,
This glorious Kings immortall gloire difplay.
Tell how he doeth in tender yearis effay
Aboue his age with fkill our arts to blaife.
Tell how he doeth with gratitude repay
The crowne he wan for his deferued praife.
    Tell how of *Ioue*, of *Mars*, but more of *God*
    The gloire and grace he hath proclaimed abrod.

M. W. F.

SONNET.

C AN goldin *Titan* fhyning bright at morne
    For light of Torchis, caft ane greater fhaw ?
    Can *Thunder* reard the heicher for a horne ?
Craks *Cannons* louder, thoght ane *Cok* fould craw ?
Can our wēake breath help *Boreas* for to blaw ?
Can *Candill* lowe giue fyre a greater heit ?
Can quhyteft *Svvans* more quhyter mak the *Snavv* ?
Can *Virgins* teares augment the *VVinters* weit ?
Helps pyping *Pan Apollos* Mufique fweit ?
Can *Fountanis* fmall the *Ocean fea* increffe ?
No, they augment the greater nocht a quhcit :
Bot they them felues appears to grow the leffe.
  So (worthy Prince) thy works fall mak the knawin.
  Ours helps not thyne : we fteynzie bot our awin.

A. M.

De huius Libri Auĉtore, Herculis
Rolloci conieĉtura.

Q *Vifquis es, entheus hic exit quo Auĉtore libellus,*
    (Nam liber Auĉtorem conticet ipfe fuum)
    Dum quonam ingenio meditor, genioque fubaĉtus,
    Maiora humanis viribus ifta canas :
Teque adeo qui fis expendo : aut Diuus es, inquam,
    Aut a Diuum aliquis forte fecundus homo.
Nil fed habet fimile aut Diuis, aut terra fecundum :
    Quanquam illis Reges proximus ornat honos.
Aut opus hoc igitur humano femine nati
    Nullius, aut hoc fic Regis oportet opus.

ACROSTICHON.I Nsigne Auctoris vetuit præfigere nomen
A uctoris cuncta pectus vacuum ambitione.
C uius præclaras laudes, heroica facta,
O mnigenasque animi dotes, et pectora verè
B elligera, exornat cœlestis gratia Musæ.
V era ista omnino est virtus, virtuteque maior
S ublimis regnat generoso in pectore Christus.
S cottia fortunata nimis bona si tua nosses
EX imij vatis, plectrum qui pollice docto
T emperat, et Musas regalem inducit in aulam:
V icturus post fata diu: Nam fama superstes
S emper erit, semper florebit gloria vatis.

Pa. Ad. Ep. Sanct.

EIVSDEM AD LECTOREM
EPIGRAMMA.

SI quæras quis sit tam compti carminis auctor,
    Auctorem audebis Musa negare tuum?
Ille quidem vetuit, cui te parere necesse est:
    Quis tantum in Diuas obtinet imperium?
Cui parent Musæ, Phœbus quo vate superbit,
    Et capiti demit laurea serta suo.
Cui lauri, et sceptri primi debentur honores,
    Cui multa cingit laude tyara caput.
Quo duce spes certa est diuisis orbe Britannis,
    Haud diuisa iterum regna futura duo.
Progenies Regum, Regnorumque vnicus hæres,
    Scilicet obscurus delituisse potest!

ANE QVADRAIN OF
ALEXANDRIN VERSE.

Mmortall Gods, fen I with pen and Poets airt [fmall,
 So willingly hes fervde you, though my fkill be
 I pray then euerie one of you to help his pairt,
In graunting this my fute, which after follow fhall.

SONNET. 1.

IRST *Ioue*, as greateft God aboue the reft,
 Graunt thou to me a pairt of my defyre :
 That when in verfe of thee I write my beft,
This onely thing I earneftly requyre,
That thou my veine Poetique fo infpyre,
As they may fuirlie think, all that it reid,
When I defcryue thy might and thundring fyre,
That they do fee thy felf in verie deid
From heauen thy greateft *Thunders* for to leid,
And fyne upon the *Gyants* heads to fall :
Or cumming to thy *Semele* with fpeid
In *Thunders* leaft, at her requeft and call :
 Or throwing *Phaethon* downe from heauen to eard.
 With threatning thunders, making monftrous reard.

SONNET. 2.

Pollo nixt, affift me in a parte,
 Sen vnto *Ioue* thou fecound art in might,
 That when I do defcryue thy fhyning Carte,
The Readers may efteme it in their fight.
And graunt me als, thou worlds ô onely light,
That when I lyke for fubiect to deuyfe
To wryte, how as before thy countenaunce bright
The yeares do ftand, with feafons dowble twyfe.
That fo I may defcryue the verie guyfe
Thus by thy help, of yeares wherein we liue :
As Readers fyne may fay, heir furely lyes,
Of feafons fowre, the glaffe and picture viue.
 Grant als, that fo I may my verfes warpe,
 As thou may play them fyne vpon thy Harpe.

SONNET. 3.

AND firſt, ô *Phœbus*, when I do deſcriue [flowris,
The *Springtyme* ſproutar of the herbes and
Whome with in rank none of the foure do ſtriue,
But neareſt thee do ſtande all tymes and howris:
Graunt Readers may eſteme, they ſie the ſhowris,
Whoſe balmie dropps ſo ſoftlie dois diſtell,
Which watrie cloudds in meſure ſuche downe powris,
As makis the herbis, and verie earth to ſmell
With ſauours ſweit, fra tyme that onis thy ſell
The vapouris ſoftlie ſowkis with ſmyling cheare,
VVhilks ſyne in cloudds are keiped cloſs and well,
VVhill vehement *Winter* come in tyme of yeare.
   Graunt, when I lyke the *Springtyme* to diſplaye.
   That Readers think they ſie the Spring alwaye.

.

SONNET. 4

AND graunt that I may ſo viuely put in verſe
The *Sommer*, when I lyke theirof to treat:
As when in writ I do theirof reherſe,
Let Readers think they ſele the burning heat,
And graithly ſee the earth, for lacke of weit,
With withering drouth and Sunne ſo gaigged all,
As for the graſſe on ſeild, the duſt in ſtreit
Doth ryſe and flee aloft, long or it fall.
Yea, let them think, they heare the ſong and call,
Which *Floras* wingde muſicians maks to ſound.
And that to taſte, and ſmell, beleue they ſhall
Delicious fruictis, whilks in that tyme abound.
   And ſhortly, all their ſenſes ſo bereaued,
   As eyes and earis, and all may be deceaued.

SONNET. 5.

OR when I lyke my pen for to imploy
    Of fertile *Harveſt* in the deſcription trew :
    Let.Readers think, they inſtantly conuoy
The buſie ſhearers for to reap their dew,
By cutting rypeſt cornes with hookes anew :
Which cornes their heauy heads did dounward bow,
Els ſeking earth againe, from whence they grew,
And vnto *Ceres* do their ſeruice vow.
Let Readers alſo ſurely think and trow,
They ſee the painfull *Vigneron* pull the grapes :
Firſt tramping them, and after preſſing now
The greneſt cluſters gathered into heapes.
    Let then the *Harveſt* ſo viue to them appeare,
    As if they ſaw both cornes and cluſters neare.

SONNET. 6.

BVT let them think, in verie deid they feill,
    When as I do the *VVinters* ſtormes vnfolde,
    The bitter froſts, which waters dois congeill
In *VVinter* ſeaſon, by a pearſing colde.
And that they heare the whiddering *Boreas* bolde,
With hiddeous hurling, rolling Rocks from hie.
Or let them think, they ſee god *Saturne* olde,
Whoſe hoarie haire owercouering earth, maks flie
The lytle birds in flocks, fra tyme they ſee
The earth and all with ſtormes of ſnow owercled :
Yea let them think, they heare the birds that die,
Make piteous mone, that *Saturnes* hairis are ſpred.
    Apollo, graunt thir foirſaid ſuitis of myne,
    All fyue I ſay, that thou may crowne me ſyne.

SONNET. 7.

AND when I do defcriue the *Oceans* force,
  Graunt fyne, ô *Neptune*, god of feas profound,
  That readars think on leebord, and on dworce,
And how the Seas owerflowed this maffiue round :
Yea, let them think, they heare a ftormy found,
Which threatnis wind, and darknes come at hand :
And water in their fhipps fyne to abound,
By weltring waues, lyke hyeft towres on land.
Then let them thinke their fhipp now low on fand,
Now climmes and fkippes to top of rageing feas,
Now downe to hell, when fhippmen may not ftand,
But lifts their hands to pray thee for fome eas.
  Syne let them think thy *Trident* doth it calme,
  Which maks it cleare and fmothe lyke glas or alme.

SONNET. 8.

AND graunt the lyke when as the fwimming fort
  Of all thy fubiects fkaled I lift declare :
  As *Triton* monfter with a manly port,
Who drownd the *Troyan* trumpetour moft raire :
As *Marmaids* wyfe, who wepis in wether faire :
And marvelous *Monkis*, I meane *Monkis* of the fee.
Bot what of monfters, when I looke and ftaire
On wounderous heapes of fubiectis feruing the ?
As whailes fo huge, and *Sea eylis* rare, that be
Myle longs, in crawling cruikis of fixtie pace :
And *Daulphins*, *Seahorfe*. *Selchs* with oxin ee,
And *Merfwynis*, *Pertrikis* als of fifhes race.
  In fhort, no fowle doth flie, nor beaft doth go,
  But thow haft fifhes lyke to them and mo.

SONNET. 9.

O Dreidfull *Pluto*, brother thrid to *Ioue*,
  With *Proferpin*, thy wife, the quene of hell
  My fute to yow is, when I like to loaue
The ioyes that do in *Elife* field excell :
Or when I like great *Tragedies* to tell :
Or flyte, or murne my *fate :* or wryte with feare
The plagues ye do fend furth with *Diræ* fell.
Let Readers think, that both they fee and heare
Alecto, threatning *Turnus* fifter deare :
And heare *Celænos* wings, with *Harpyes* all :
And fee dog *Cerberus* rage with hiddeous beare,
And all that did *A Eneas* once befall.
    When as he paft throw all thofe dongeons dim,
    The forefaid feilds fyne vifited by him.

SONNET. 10.

O Furious *Mars*, thow warlyke fouldiour bold,
  And hardy *Pallas*, goddefs ftout and graue :
  Let Reidars think, when combats manyfold
I do defcriue, they fee two champions braue,
With armies huge approching to refaue
Thy will, with cloudds of duft into the air.
Syne Phifers, Drummes, and Trumpets cleir do craue
The pelmell chok with larum loude alwhair,
Then nothing hard but gunnis, and ratling fair
Of fpeares, and clincking fwords with glaunce fo cleir,
As if they foght in fkyes, then wrangles thair
Men killd, vnkilld, whill *Parcas* breath reteir.
    There lyes the venquifht wailing fore his chaunce :
    There lyes the victor, rewing els the daunce.

B

SONNET. 11.

ANd at your handis I earneftly do craue,
    O facound *Mercure*, with the *Mufes* nyne,
        That for conducting guyde I may you haue,
Afwell vnto my pen, as my Ingyne.
Let Readers think, thy eloquence deuyne
O *Mercure*, in my Poems doth appeare :
And that *Parnaffis* flowing fountaine fyne
Into my works doth fhyne lyke criftall cleare.
O *Mufes*, let them think that they do heare
Your voyces all into my verfe refound.
And that your vertewis finguler and feir
May wholly all in them be alfo found.
    Of all that may the perfyte Poems make,
    I pray you let my verfes haue no lake.

SONNET. 12.

IN fhort, you all forenamed gods I pray
    For to concur with one accord and will,
        That all my works may perfyte be alway :
Which if ye doe, then fweare I for to fill
My works immortall with your praifes ftill :
I fhall your names eternall euer fing,
I fhall tread downe the graffe on *Parnafs* hill
By making with your names the world to ring :
I fhall your names from all obliuion bring.
I lofty *Virgill* fhall to life reftoir,
My fubiects all fhalbe of heauenly thing,
How to delate the gods immortals gloir.
Effay me once, and if ye find me fwerue,
Then thinke, I do not graces fuch deferue.

FINIS.

THE VRANIE

tranſlated.

✻ *To the fauorable*
Reader

HAuing oft reuolued, and red ouer (fauorable Reader) the booke and Poems of the deuine and Illuſter Poëte, *Saluſt du Bartas*, I was moued by the oft reading and peruſing of them, with a reſtles and lofty deſire, to preas to attaine to the like vertue. But ſen (alas) God, by nature hathe refuſed me the like lofty and quick ingyne, and that my dull *Muſe*, age, and Fortune, had refuſed me the lyke ſkill and learning, I was conſtrained to haue refuge to the ſecound, which was, to doe what lay in me, to ſet forth his praiſe, ſen I could not merite the lyke my ſelf. Which I thought, I could not do ſo well, as by publiſhing ſome worke of his, to this yle of *Brittain* (ſwarming full of quick ingynes,) aſwell as they ar made manifeſt already to France. But knowing my ſelf to vnſkilfull and groſſe, to tranſlate any of his heauenly and learned works, I almoſt left it of, and was aſhamed of that opinion alſo. Whill at the laſt, preferring foolehardines and a good intention, to an vtter diſpaire and ſleuth, I reſolued vnaduyſedly to aſſay the tranſlating in my language of the eaſieſt and ſhorteſt of all his difficile, and prolixed Poems: to wit, the *Vranie* or heauenlye Muſe, which, albeit it be not well tranſlated, yet hope I, ye will excuſe me (fauorable Reader) ſen I neither ordained it, nor auowes it for a iuſt tranſlation : but onely ſet it forth, to the end, that, albeit the Prouerb ſaith, that foolehardines proceeds of ignorance, yet ſome quick ſprited man of this yle, borne vnder the ſame, or as

happie a Planet, as *Du Bartas* was, might by the reading of it, bee moued to tranflate it well, and beft,
where I haue bothe euill, and worft broyled it.

For that caufe, I haue put in, the French on the
one fide of the leif, and my blocking on the other:
noght thereby to giue proofe of my iuft tranflating, but
by the contrair, to let appeare more plainly to the
forefaid reader, wherin I haue erred, to the effect, that
with leffe difficulty he may efcape thofe fnares wherin
I haue fallen. I muft alfo defire you to bear with it,
albeit it be replete with innumerable and intolerable
faultes : fic as, Ryming in tearmes, and dyuers others,
whilkis ar forbidden in my owne treatife of the Art of
Poëfie, in the hinder end of this booke, I muft, I fay,
praye you for to appardone mee, for three caufes.
Firft, becaufe that tranflations are limitat, and re-
ftraind in fome things, more than free inuentions are,
Therefore reafoun would, that it had more libertie in
others. Secoundlie, becaufe I made noght my treatife
of that intention, that eyther I, or any others behoued
aftricktly to follow it : but that onely it fhould fhew
the perfection of Poefie, whereunto fewe or none can
attaine. Thirdlye, becaufe, that (as I fhewe alreadye)
I avow it not for a iuft tranflation. Befydes that I
haue but ten feete in my lyne, where he hath twelue,
and yet tranflates him lyne by lyne. Thus not doub-
ting, fauorable Reader, but you will accept my
intention and trauellis in good parte,
(fen I requyre no farder,) I
bid you faire well.

✻

✻ ✻ ✻

✻ ✻ ✻ ✻ ✻

✻ ✻ ✻

✻

L'VRANIE, OV MVSE
CELESTE.

E n'eſtoy point encor en l'Auril de
mon aage,
Qu' vn deſir d'affranchir mon renom
du treſpas,
Chagrin, me faiſoit perdre et repos,
et repas,
Par le braue proiet de maint ſçauant
ouurage.

Mais comme vn pelerin, qui ſur le tard, rencontre
Vn fourchu carrefour, douteux, s'arreſte court :
Et d'eſprit, non des pieds, de çà de là diſcourt,
Par les diuers chemins, que la Lune luy monſtre.

Parmi tant de ſentiers qui, fleuris, ſe vont rendre
Sur le mont, où Phœbus guerdonne les beaux vers
De l'honneur immortel des lauriers tout-iour verds,
Ie demeuroy confus, ne ſçachant lequel prendre.

Tantoſt i'entreprenoy d'orner la Grecque Scene
D'vn veſtement Francois. Tantoſt dvn vers plus haut,
Hardi, i'enſanglantoy le François eſchafaut
Des Tyrans d'Ilion, de Thebes, de Mycene.

Ie conſacroy tantoſt à l'Aonide bande
L'Histoire des Francois : et ma ſainĉte fureur
Deſmentant à bon droit la trop commune erreur.
Faiſoit le Mein Gaulois, non la Seine Alemande.

Tantoſt ie deſſeignoy dvne plume flateuſe
Le los non merité des Rois et grands Seigneurs :
Et, pour me voir bien toſt riche d'or, et d honneurs,
D'vn cœur bas ie rendoy mercenaire ma Muſe.

Et tandis ie vouloy chanter le fils volage
De la molle Cypris, et le mal doux-amer,

THE VRANIE, OR HEA-
VENLY MVSE.

S Carce was I yet in fpringtyme of my
    years,
    When greening great for fame aboue
      my pears
    Did make me lofe my wonted chere
      and reft,
    Effaying learned works with curious
      breft.
But as the *Pilgrim*, who for lack of light,
Cumd on the parting of two wayes at night,
He ftays affone, and in his mynde doeth caft,
What way to take while Moonlight yet doth laft.
So I amongft the paths vpon that hill,
Where *Phœbus* crowns all verfes euer ftill
Of endles praife, with *Laurers* always grene,
Did ftay confufde, in doubt what way to mene.
I whyles effaide the *Grece* in Frenche to praife,
Whyles in that toung I gaue a lufty glaife
For to defcryue the *Troian* Kings of olde,
And them that *Thebes* and *Mycens* crowns did holde.
And whiles I had the ftorye of Fraunce elected,
Which to the Mufes I fhould haue directed :
My holy furie with confent of nane,
Made frenche the *Mein*, and nowyfe dutche the *Sein*.
Whiles thought I to fet foorth with flattring pen :
The praife vntrewe of Kings and noble men,
And that I might both golde and honours haue,
With courage baffe I made my Mufe a flaue.
And whyles I thought to fing the fickle boy
Of *Cypris* foft, and loues to-fwete anoy,   ·

Que les plus beaux esprits souffrent pour trop aimer,
Difcours, où me poufsoit ma nature, et mon aage.
    Or tandis qu' inconftant ie ne me puis refoudre,
De çà, de là poufsé d vn vent ambitieux,
Vne fainte beauté fe prefente à mes yeux,
Fille, comme ie croy, du grand Dieu lance-foudre.
    Sa face eft angelique, angelique fon gefte,
Son difcours tout diuin, et tout parfait fon corps :
Et fa bouche à neuf-voix imite en fes accords
Le fon harmonieux de la dance celefte.
    Son chef eft honoré d'vne riche couronne
Faite à fept plis, gliffans d vn diuers mouuement,
Sur chacun de fes plis fe tourne obliquement
Ie ne fçay quel rondeau, qui fur nos chefs raionne.
    Le premier eft de plomb, et d eftain le deuxiefme.
Le troifiefme d acier, le quart d or iauniffant,
Le quint eft compofé d electre palliffant,
Le fuyuant de Mercure, et d argent le feptiefme.
    Son corps est affublé d vne mante azurée,
Semée haut et bas d vn million de feux,
Qui d vn bel art fans art diftinctement confus,
Decorent de leurs rais cefte beauté facrée.
    Icy luit le grand Char, icy flambe la Lyre,
Icy la Poufsiniere, icy les clairs Beffons,
Icy le Trebufchet, icy les deux Poiffons,
Et mille autres brandons que ie ne puis defcrire.
    Ie fuis [dit elle alors] cefte docte VRANIE,
Qui fur les gonds aftrez tranfporte les humains,
Faifant voir à leurs yeux, et toucher à leurs mains,
Ce que la Cour celefte et contemple et manie.
    Ie quinte-efsence l ame : et fay que le Poete
Se furmontant foy mefme, enfonce vn haut difcours,
Qui, diuin, par l oreille attire les plus fourds,
Anime les rochers, et les fleuues arrefte.
    Agreable eft le fonde mes doctes germaines :
Mais leur gofier, qui peut terre et ciel enchanter,
Ne me cede pas moins en l art de bien chanter,
Qu'au Rofsignol l'Oifon, les Pies aux Syrenes.   [aifle
    Pren moy donques pour guide : efleue au ciel ton

To lofty fprits that are therewith made blynd,
To which difcours my nature and age inclynd.
But whill I was in doubt what way to go,
With wind ambitious toffed to and fro :
A holy beuty did to mee appeare,
The *Thundrers* daughter feeming as fhe weare.
Her porte was Angellike with Angels face,
With comely fhape and toung of heauenly grace :
Her nynevoced mouth refembled into found
The daunce harmonious making heauen refound.
Her head was honorde with a coftly crown,
Seuinfolde and round, to dyuers motions boun :
On euery folde I know not what doth glance,
Aboue our heads into a circuler dance.
The firft it is of Lead, of Tin the nixt,   The feuin
The third of Stele, the fourth of Gold vnmixt,   Planets.
The fyfth is made of pale Electre light,
The fixt of Mercure, feuint of Siluer bright.
Her corps is couured with an Afure gowne,   Firnament.
Where thoufand fires ar fowne both vp and downe :
Whilks with an arte, but arte, confufde in order,   Fixed
Dois with their beames decore thereof the border.   Starres.
Heir fhynes the Charlewain, there the Harp giues light,
And heir the Seamans ftarres, and there Twinnis bright,
And heir the Ballance, there the Fifhes twaine,
With thoufand other fyres, that pas my braine.
I am faid fhe, that learned VRANIE,
That to the Starres tranfports humanitie,
And maks men fee and twiche with hands and ene
It that the heauenly court contempling bene.
I quint-effence the Poets foule fo well,
While he in high difcours excede him fell,
Who by the eare the deafeft doeth allure,
Reuiues the rocks, and ftayes the floods for fure.   Nyne
The tone is pleafaunt of my * fifters deir :   Mufes.
Yet though their throts make heauen and earth admire,
They yeld to me no leffe in finging well,
Then Pye to Syraine, goofe to Nightingell.
Take me for guyde, lyft vp to heauen thy wing

Saluſte, chante moy du Tout-puiſsant l honneur,
Et remontant le luth du Ieſſean ſonneur,
Courageux, broſſe apres la couronne eternelle.

Ie ne puis d vn œil ſec, voir mes ſœurs maquerelles,
Des amoreuz François, dont les mignards eſcrits [cris,
Sont pleins de ſeints ſouſpirs, de ſeints pleurs, de ſeints
D'impudiques diſcours, et de vaines querelles.

Ie ne puis d vn œil ſec voir que l on mette en vente,
Nos diuines chanſons : et que d vn flateur vers,
Pour gaigner la faueur des Princes plus peruers,
Vn Commode, vn Neron, vn Caligule on vante.

Mais, ſur tout, ie ne puis ſans ſouſpirs et ſans larmes
Voir les vers employez contre l autheur des vers :
Ie ne puis voir battu le Roy de l'vniuers
De ſes propres ſoldats, et de ſes propres armes.

L'homme a les yeux ſillez de nuits Cimmeriennes,
Et s'il a quelque bien, tant ſoit peu precieux,
Par differentes mains il l a receu des cieux :
Mais Dieu ſeul nous apprend les chanſons Delphiennes.

Tout art s'apprend par art : la ſeule Poeſie
Est vn pur don celeſte : et nul ne peut gouſter
Le miel, que nous faiſons de Pinde degoutter
S'il n'a d'vn ſacré feu la poitrine ſaiſie.

De ceſte ſource vient, que maints grands perſonnage
Conſommez en ſçauoir, voire en proſe diſerts,
Se trauaillent en vain à compoſer des vers :
Et qu'vn ieune apprenti fait de plus beaux ouurages.

De là vient que iadis le chantre Meonide,
Combien que mendiant, et ſans maiſtre, et ſans yeux,
A vaincu par ſes vers les nouueaux, et les vieux,
Chantant ſi bien Vlyſſe, et le preux Aeacide.

De là vient qu'vn Naſon ne peut parler en proſe,
De là vient que Dauid mes chants ſi toſt aprit,
De paſteur fait Poëte, et que maint ieune eſprit [poſe.
Ne ſçachant point noſtre art, fuyuant noſtre art com-

Recherche nuiƈt et iour les ondes Caſtalides :
Regrimpe nuiƈt et iour contre le roc Beſſon :
Sois diſciple d'Homere, et du ſainƈt nourriſſon
D'Ande, l'heureux ſeiour des vierges Pierides.

O *Saluſt*, Gods immortals honour ſing :
And bending higher *Dauids* Lute in tone,
With courage ſeke yon endles crowne abone.
I no wais can, vnwet my cheekes, beholde
My ſiſters made by Frenchemen macquerels olde,
Whoſe mignarde writts, but faynd lamenting vaine,
And fayned teares and ſhamles tales retaine.
But weping neither can I ſee them ſpyte
Our heauenly verſe, when they do nothing wryte,
But Princes flattery that ar tyrants rather
Then *Nero, Commode,* or *Caligule* ather.
But ſpecially but ſobbes I neuer ſhall
Se verſe beſtowde gainſt him made verſes all,
I can not ſee his proper ſoldiers ding
With his owne armes him that of all is King.
Mans eyes are blinded with *Cimmerien* night :
And haue he any good, beit neuer ſo light,
From heauen, by mediat moyens, he it reaches,
Bot only God the *Delphiens* ſong vs teaches.
All art is learned by art, this art alone
It is a heauenly gift : no fleſh nor bone
Can preiſ the honnie we from *Pinde* diſtill,
Except with holy ſyre his breeſt we fill.
From that ſpring flowes, that men of ſpeciall choſe,
Conſumde in learning, and perfyte in proſe,
For to make verſe in vaine dois trauell take.
When as a prentiſe fairer works will make.
That made that *Homer*, who a ſongſter bene,
Albeit a beggar, lacking maſter, and ene,
Exceded in his verſe both new and olde,
In ſinging *Vliſs* and *Achilles* bolde.
That made that *Naſo* noght could ſpeak but verſe,
That *Dauid* made my ſongs ſo ſone reherſe,
Of paſtor Poët made., yea youngmen whyles
Vnknowing our art, yet by our art compyles.
Seke night and day *Caſtalias* waltring waas,
Climme day and night the twinrocks of *Parnaas* :
Be *Homers* ſkoller, and his, was born in *Ande,*   *Virgill*
The happie dwelling place of all our bande.

Lis tant que tu voudras, volume apres volume,
Les liures de Pergame, et de la grande cité,
Qui du nom d'Alexandre a fon nom emprunté :
Exerce inceffamment et ta langue, et ta plume.

   Ioin tant que tu voudras, pour vn carme bien faire
L'obfcure nuiċt au iour, et le iour â la nuiċt,
Si ne pourras tu point cueillir vn digne fruit
D'vn fi fafcheux trauail, fi Pallas t'eft contraire.   [forte.

   Car du tout hors de l homme it fault que l homme
Sil veut faire des vers qui facent tefte aux ans :
Il fault qu entre nos mains il fequeftre fes fens :
Il fault qu vn faint ecftafe an plus haut ciel l'emporte.

   D autant que tout ainfi que la fureur humaine
Rend l homme moins qu humain : la diuine fureur
Rend l homme plus grand qu homme : et d vne fainċte
Sur le ciel porte-feux à fon gré le promeine.   [erreur

   Ceft d vn fi facré lieu que les diuins poëtes
Nous apportent ça bas de fi doċtes propos,
Et des vers non fuiets au pouuoir d Atropos,
Truchemens de Nature, et du Ciel interpretes.

   Les vrais Poëtes font tels que la cornemufe,
Qui pleine de vent fonne, et vuide perd le fon :
Car leur fureur durant, dure auffi leur chanfon :
Et fi la fureur ceffe, auffi ceffe leur Mufe.

   Puis donques que les vers ont au ciel pris naiffance,
Efprits vrayment diuins, aurez vous bien le cœur
De prononcer vn vers et profane, et moqueur
Contre cil, qui conduit des cieux aftrez la danfe ?

   Serez vous tant ingrats, que de rendre vos plumes
Miniftres de la chair, et ferues de peché ?
Tout-iour donques fera voftre ftyle empefché
A remplir, menfongers, de fonges vos volumes ?

   Ferez-vous, ô trompeurs, tout-iour d'vn diable vn Ange?
Fendrez vous tout-iour l'air de vos amoureux cris ?
Hé ! n'orra on iamais dans vos doċtes efcrits
Retentir haut et clair du grand Dieu la louange ?

   Ne vous fuffit il pas de fentir dans voftre ame
Le Cyprien brandon, fans que plus effrontez
Qu'vne Lays publique, encor vous euentez

How oft thou lykes reid ouer booke efter booke,
The bookes of *Troy*, and of that towne which tooke
Her name from *Alexander* Monark then,   Alexandria
Exerce but ceafe thy toung and eke thy pen.
Yea, if to make good verfe thou hes fic cure,
Ioyne night and day, and day to night obfcure,
Yet fhall thou not the worthy frute reape fo
Of all thy paines, if *Pallas* be thy fo.
For man from man muft wholly parted be,
If with his age, his verfe do well agree.
Amongft our hands, he muft his witts refing,
A holy trance to higheft heauen him bring.
For euen as humane fury maks the man.   √
Les then the man : So heauenly fury can
Make man pas man, and wander in holy mift,
Vpon the fyrie heauen to walk at lift.
Within that place the heauenly Poëts fought   √
Their learning, fyne to vs heare downe it brought,
With verfe that ought to *Atropos* no dewe,
Dame *Naturs* trunchmen, heauens interprets trewe, ·
For Poets right are lyke the pype alway,
Who full doth found, and empty ftayes to play : √
Euen fo their fury lafting, lafts their tone,
Their fury ceaft, their Mufe doth ftay affone.
Sen verfe did then in heauen firft bud and blume,
If ye be heauenly, how dar ye prefume
A verfe prophane, and mocking for to fing
Gainft him that leads of ftarrie heauens the ring?
Will ye then fo ingrately make your pen,
A flaue to finne, and ferue but flefhly men ?
Shall ftill your brains be bufied then to fill
With dreames, ô dreamers, euery booke and bill?
Shall Satan ftill be God for your behoue?
Still will ye riue the aire with cryes of loue?
And fhall there neuer into your works appeare,
The praife of God, refounding loud and cleare?
Suffifis it noght ye feele into your hairt
The *Ciprian* torche, vnles more malapairt
Then *Lais* commoun quean, ye blow abrod

Par le monde abuſé voſtre impudique flamme ?
   Ne vous ſuffit il pas de croupir en delices,
Sans que vous corrompiez, par vos nombres charmeurs,
Du lecteur indiſcret les peu-conſtantes mœurs,
Luy faiſant embraſer pour les vertus les vices ?
   Les tons, nombres, et chants, dont ſe fait l'harmonie,
Qui rend le vers ſi beau, ont ſur nous tel pouuoir,
Que les plus durs Catons ils peuuent eſmouuoir,
Agitant nos eſprits d'vne douce manie.
   Ainſi que le cachet dedans la cire forme
Preſque vn autre cachet, le Poete ſçauant,
Va ſi bien dans nos cœurs ſes paſſions grauant,
Que preſque l'auditeur en l'auteur ſe tranſſorme.
   Car la ſorce des vers, qui ſecrettement gliſſe,
Par des ſecrets conduits, dans nos entendemens,
Y empreint tous les bons et mauuais mouuemens,
Qui ſont repreſentez par vn docte artifice.
   Et c'eſt pourquoy Platon hors de ſa Republique
Chaſſoit les eſcriuains, qui ſouloient par leurs vers
Rendre meſchans les bons, plus peruers les peruers,
Sapans par leurs beaux mots l'honneſteté publique.
   Non ceux qui dans leurs chants marioient les beaux
Auec les beaux ſuiets : ore entonnans le los   [termes
Du iuſte ſoudroyeur : ore d'vn ſaint propos,
Seruans aux deſuoyez et de guides et d'Hermes.
   Profanes eſcriuains, voſtre impudique rime,
Eſt cauſe, que l'on met nos chantres mieux-diſans
Au rang des baſteleurs, des boufons, des plaiſans :
Et qu'encore moins qu'eux le peuple les eſtime.
   Vos ſaites de Clion vne Thais impure :
D'Helicon vn bordeau : vous ſaites impudens,
Par vos laſcifs diſcours, que les peres prudens
Deffendent à leurs fils des carmes la lecture.
   Mais ſi ſoulans aux pieds la deité volage,
Qui blece de ces traits vos idolatres cœurs,
Vous vouliez employer vos plus ſainctes ſureurs
A ſaire voir en France vn ſacré-ſainct ouurage.
   Chacun vous priſeroit, comme eſtans ſecretaires,
Et miniſtres ſacrez du Roy de l vniuers.

But fhame, athort the world, your fhameles god?
Abufers, ftaikes it not to lurk in luft,
Without ye fmit with charming nombers iuft
The fickle maners of the reader flight,
In making him embrace, for day, the night?
The harmony of nomber tone and fong,
That makes the verfe fo fair, it is fo ftrong √
Ouer vs, as hardeft *Catos* it will moue,
With fpreits aflought, and fweete tranfported loue.
For as into the wax the feals imprent
Is lyke a feale, right fo the Poët gent,
Doeth graue fo viue in vs his paffions ftrange,
As maks the reader, halfe in author change.
For verfes force is fic, that foftly flydes
Throw fecret poris, and in our fences bydes,
As makes them haue both good and euill imprented,
Which by the learned works is reprefented.
And therefore *Plato*s common wealth did pack
None of thefe Poëts, who by verfe did make
The goodmen euill, and the wicked worfe,
Whofe pleafaunt words betraied the publick corfe.
Not thofe that in their fongs good tearmes alwaife
Ioynd with fair Thems: whyles thundring out the praife
Of God, iuft Thundrer: whyles with holy fpeache,
Lyke *Hermes* did the way to ftrayers teache.
Your fhameles rymes, are caufe, ô Scrybes prophane,
That in the lyke opinion we remaine
With Iuglers, buffons, and that foolifh feames:
Yea les then them, the people of vs efteames.
For *Clio* ye put *Thais* vyle in vre,
For *Helicon* a bordell.   Ye procure
By your lafciuious fpeache, that fathers fage
Defends verfe reading, to their yonger age.
But lightleing * yon fleing godhead flight,   Cupide
Who in Idolatrous breafts his darts hath pight.
If that ye would imploy your holy traunce,
To make a holy hallqwde worke in Fraunce:
Then euery one wolde worthy fcribes you call,
And holy feruants to the King of all.

Chacun reuereroit comme oracles vos vers :
Et les grands commettroient en vos mains leurs affaires.
    La liaifon des vers fut iadis inuentee
Seulement pour traitter les myfteres facrez
Auec plus de refpect : et de long temps apres
Par les carmes ne fut autre chofe chantee.
    Ainfi mon grand Dauid fur la corde tremblante
De fon luth tout-diuin ne fonne rien que Dieu.
Ainfi le conducteur de l'exercite Hebrieu,
Sauué des rouges flots, le los du grand Dieu chante.
    Ainfi Iudith, Delbore, au milieu des genf d'armes,
Ainfi Iob, Ieremie, accablez de douleurs,
D vn carme bigarré de cent mille couleurs
Defcriuoient faintement leurs ioyes, et leurs larmes.
    Voyla pourquoy Satan, qui fin se tranffigure
En Ange de clarté pour nous enforceler,
Ses preftres et fes dieux faifoit iadis parler,
Non d vne libre language, ains par nombre, et mefure.
    Ainfi, fous Apollon la folle Phœmonoe
En hexametres vers fes oracles chantoit :
Et, par douteux propos, cauteleufe affrontoit
Non le Grec feulement, ains l'Ibere, et l'Eoe.
    Ainfi l antique voix en Dodone adorée,
Aefculape, et Ammon en vers prophetizoient,
Les Sibylles en vers le futur predifoient,
Et les preftres prioient en oraifon nombrée.
    Ainfi Line, Hefiode, et celuy dont la lyre
Oreilloit, comme on dit, les rocs, et les forefts,
Oferent autrefois les plus diuins fecrets
De leur profond fçauoir en doctes vers efcrire.
    Vous qui tant defirez vos fronts de laurier ceindre,
Où pourriez vous trouuer vn champ plus fpacieux,
Que le los de celuy qui tient le frein des cieux,
Qui fait trembler les monts, qui fait l'Erebe craindre ?
    Ce fuiet est de vray la Corne d abondance,
C'eft vn grand magazin riche en difcours faconds,
C'eft vn grand Ocean, qui n'a riue, ny fonds,
Vn furjon immortel de diuine eloquence.
    L'humble fuiet ne peut qu'humble difcours produire :

Echone your verſe for oracles wolde take,
And great men of their counſell wolde you make.
The verſes knitting was found out and tryit,
For ſinging only holy myſteries by it
With greater grace.   And efter that, were pend
Longtyme no verſe, but for that only end.
Euen ſo my *Dauid* on the trembling ſtrings
Of heauenly harps, Gods only praiſe he ſings.
Euen ſo the leader of the *Hebrevv* hoſt
Gods praiſe did ſing vpon the Redſea coſt
So *Iudith* and *Delbor* in the ſoldiers throngs,
So *Iob* and *Ieremie*, preaſt with woes and wrongs,
Did right deſcryue their ioyes, their woes and torts,
In variant verſe of hundreth thouſand ſorts.
And therefore crafty Sathan, who can ſeame
An Angell of light, to witch vs in our dreame,
He cauſde his gods and preeſts of olde to ſpeake
By nomber and meaſure, which they durſt not breake.
So fond *Phœmonoë* vnder *Apollos* wing,
Her oracles *Hexameter* did ſing :
With doubtſum talk ſhe craftely begylde,
Not only *Grece*, but *Spaine* and *Indes* ſhe ſylde.
That olde voce ſerude in *Dodon*, ſpak in verſe,
So *Æſculap* did, and ſo did *Ammon* fearſe,
So *Sybills* tolde in verſe, what was to come :
The Preeſts did pray by nombers, all and ſome.
So *Heſiod*, *Line*, and he* whoſe Lute they ſay, Orpheus
Made rocks and forreſts come to heare him play,
Durſt well their heauenly ſecrets all diſcloes,
In learned verſe, that ſoftly ſlydes and goes.
O ye that wolde your browes with *Laurel* bind,
What larger feild I pray you can you find,
Then is his praiſe, who brydles heauens moſt cleare,
Maks mountaines tremble, and howeſt hells to feare ?
That is a horne of plenty well repleat :
That is a ſtorehouſe riche, a learning ſeat.
An Ocean hudge, both lacking ſhore and ground,
Of heauenly eloquence a ſpring profound.
From ſubieĉts baſe, a baſe diſcours dois ſpring,

C

Mais le graue fuiet de foymefme produit
Graues et mafles mots : de foymefmes il luit,
Et fait le fainct honneur de fon chantre reluire.

Or donc fi vous voulez apres vos cendres viure,
N'imitez Eroftrat, qui pour viure, brufla
Le temple Ephefien : ou celuy qui moula,
Pour eftendre fon nom, vn cruel veau de cuiure.

Ne vueillez employer voftre rare artifice
A chanter la Cyprine, et fon fils emplumé :
Car il vaut beaucoup mieux n'eftre point renommé,
Que fe voir renommé pour raifon de fon vice.

Vierges font les neuf fœurs, qui dancent fur Parnaffe,
Vierge voftre Pallas : et vierge ce beau corps
Qu' vn fleuue vit changer fur les humides bords
En l'arbre tout-iour vert, qui vous cheueux enlace.

Confacrez moy pluftoft cefte rare eloquence
A chanter hautement les miracles compris
Dans le facré fueillet : et de vos beaux efprits
Verfez là, mes amis, toute la quinte-effence.   [melle
Que Chrift, comme Homme-Dieu, foit la croupe iu-
Sur qui vous fommeillez.   Que pour cheual ailé
L'Efprit du Trois-fois grand, d vn blanc pigeon voilé,
Vous face ruiffeler vne fource immortelle.

Tout ouurage excellent la memoire eternize
De ceux qui tant foit peu trauaillent apres luy :
Le Maufolee a fait viure iufquauiourd huy
Timothee, Bryace, et Scope, et Artemife.

Hiram feroit fans nom, fans la fainte afsiftance
Qu'il fit au baftiment du temple d'Ifraël.
Et fans l'Arche de Dieu l'Hebrieu Befeleel
Seroit enfeueli fous eternel filence.

Et puis que la beauté de ces rares ouurages
Fait viure apres la mort tous ceux qui les ont faits,
Combien qu'auec le temps les plus feurs foient deffaits
Par rauines, par feux, par guerres, par orages.

Penfez, ie vous fuppli, combien fera plus belle
La louange, qu heureux, ça bas vous acquerrez,
Lors que dans vos faints vers DIEV feul vous chanterez
Puis qu vn nom immortel vient de chofe immortelle.

A lofty fubiect of it felfe doeth bring
Graue words and weghtie, of it felfe diuine,
And makes the authors holy honour fhine.
If ye wolde after afhes liue, bewaire,
To do lyke *Eroftrat*, who brunt the faire
Ephefian temple, or him, to win a name,
* Who built of braffe, the crewell Calfe vntame.   Perillus
Let not your art fo rare then be defylde,
In finging *Venus* and her fethred chyide :
For better it is without renowme to be,
Then be renowmde for vyle iniquitie.
Thofe nyne are Maides, that daunce vpon *Parnaas*?
Learnd *Pallas* is a Virgin pure, lyke as
* That fair, whome waters changed on wattry banks   Daphne
Into * that tre ftill grene, your hair that hanks.   Laurell
Then confecrat that eloquence moft rair,
To fing the lofty miracles and fair
Of holy Scripture : and of your good ingyne,
Poure out, my frends, there your fift-effence fyne.
Let Chrift both God and man your Twinrock be,
Whome on ye flepe : for that *hors who did fle,   Pegasus
Speak of that *thryfe great fpreit, whofe dow moft white
Mote make your fpring flow euer with delyte.   Holyghost.
All excellent worke beare record euer fhall,
Of trauellers in it, though their paines be fmall.
The *Maufole* tombe the names did eternife
Of *Scope*, *Timotheus*, *Briace* and *Artemife*.
But *Hirams* holy help, it war vnknowne
What he in building *Izraels* Temple had fhowne,
Without Gods Ark *Befeleel* Iewe had bene
In euerlafting filence buried clene.
Then, fince the bewty of thofe works moft rare
Hath after death made liue all them that ware
Their builders : though them felues with tyme be failde,
By fpoils, by fyres, by warres, and tempefts quailde.
I pray you think, how mekle fairer fhall
Your happie name heirdowne be, when as all
Your holy verfe, great God alone fhall fing,
Since praife immortall commes of endles thing.

Ie fçay que vous direz que les antiques fables
Sont l'ame de vos chants, que ces contes diuers,
L'vn de l autre naiffans, peuuent rendre vos vers
Beaucoup plus que l'hiftoire au vulgaire admirables.

Mais où peut on trouuer chofes plus merueilleufes
Que celles de la Foy ? hé ! quel autre argument
Auec plus de tefmoins noftre raifon defment,
Qui rabat plus l'orgueil des ames curieufes ?

I'aymeroy mieux chanter la tour Affyrienne,
Que les trois monts Gregeois l'vn deffus l'autre entez
Pour dethrofner du ciel les dieux efpouuantez :
Et l'onde de Noé, que la Deucalienne.

I'aymeroy mieux chanter le changement fubite
Du Monarque d'Affur, que de l'Arcadien,
Et le viure fecond du faint Bethanien,
Que le recolement des membres d'Hippolite.

L'vn de plaire au lecteur tant feulement fe mefle,
Et l'autre feulement tafche de profiter :
Mais feul celuy là peut le laurier meriter,
Qui, fage, le profit auec le plaifir mefle.

Les plus beaux promenoirs font pres de la marine,
Et le nager plus fuer pres des riuages verds :
Et le fage Efcriuain n'efloigne dans fes vers
Le fçauoir du plaifir, le ieu de la doctrine.

Vous tiendrez donc ce rang en chantant chofes telles:
Car enfeignans autruy, vous mefmes apprendrez
La reigle de bien viure : et bien-heureux, rendrez
Autant que leurs fuiets, vos chanfons immortelles.

Laiffez moy donc à part ces fables furannées :
Mes amis, laiffez moy ceft infolent Archer,
Qui les cœurs otieux peut feulement brefcher,
Et plus ne foyent par vous les Mufes profanées.

Mais las ! en vain ie crie, en vain, las ! ie m enroue:
Car l vn, pour ne fe voir conuaincu par mon chant,
Va, comme vn fin afpic, fon oreille bouchant :
L'autre Epicurien, de mes difcours fe ioue.

L'autre pour quelque temps fe range en mon efchole
Mais le monde enchanteur foudain le me fouftrait,
Et ce difcours facré, qui les feuls bons attrait,

I know that ye will fay, the auncient rables
Decores your fongs, and that * thofe dyuers fables, Metamor
Ilk bred of other, doeth your verfes mak   phosis
More loued then ftoryes by the vulgar pack.
But where can there more wondrous things be found,
Then thofe of faith? ô fooles, what other ground,
With witnes mo, our reafons quyte improues,
Beats doun our pryde, that curious queftions moues?
I had farr rather *Babell* tower forthfett,   Ossa Pin-
Then the *thre *Grecian* hilles on others plett,   dus, and
                                                     Olympus
To pull doun gods afraide, and in my moode,
Sing *Noës* rather then *Deucalions* floode.
I had far rather fing the fuddaine change   Nabuchad
Of *Affurs* monark, then of *Arcas* ftrange.   nezer.
Of the* *Bethaniens* holy fecond liuing,   Lazarus.
Then *Hippolitts* with members glewde reuiuing.
To pleafe the Reader is the ones whole cair,
The vther for to proffite mair and mair:
But only he of *Laurell* is conding,
Who wyfely can with proffit, pleafure ming.
The faireft walking on the Sea coaft bene,
And fuireft fwimming where the braes are grene:
So, wyfe is he, who in his verfe can haue
Skill mixt with pleafure, fports with doctrine graue.
In finging kepe this order fhowen you heir,
Then ye your felf, in teaching men fhall leir
The rule of liuing well, and happely fhall
Your fongs make, as your thems immortall all.
No more into thofe oweryere lies delyte,
My freinds, caft of that infolent archer quyte,
Who only may the ydle harts furpryfe:
Prophane no more the *Mufes* with yon cryes.
But oh! in vaine, with crying am I horce:
For lo, where one, noght caring my fongs force,
Goes lyke a crafty fnaik, and ftoppes his eare:
The other godles, mocks and will not heare.
Ane other at my fchoole abydes a fpace,
While charming world withdrawe him from that place:
So that difcours, that maks good men reiofe,

Entre par vne aureille, et par l'autre s'envolle.
    Las ! ie n en voy pas vn qui ſes deux yeux deſsille
Du bandeau de Venus, et d vn profane fiel
De ſes carmes dorez ne corrompe le miel :
Bien que de bons eſprits noſtre France fourmille.
    Mais toy, mon cher mignon, que la Neufuaine ſainɛte
Qui de Pegaſe boit le ſurjon perennel,
Fit le ſacré ſonneur du los de l'Eternel,
Meſme auant que de toy ta mere fuſt enceinte :
    Bien que cest argument ſemble vne maigre lande,
Que les meilleurs eſprits ont en friche laiſsé,
Ne ſois pour l auenir de ce trauail laſsé :
Car plus la glorie eſt rare, et tant plus elle eſt grande.
    SALVSTE, ne perds cœur ſi tu vois que l Enuie
Aille abbayant, maligne, apres ton los naiſſant :
Ne crain que ſous ſes pieds elle aille tapiſſant
Les vers que tu feras, comme indignes de vie.
    Ce monſtre blece-honneur reſſemble la Maſtine,
Qui iappe contre ceux qui ſont nouueau venus,
Pardonnant toutesfois à ceux qui ſont cognus,
Curtoiſe enuers ceux cy, enuers ceux lâ mutine.
    Ce monſtre ſemble encor vne fameuſe nue,
Que le naiſſant Vulcan preſſe de toutes pars,
Pour, noire, l eſtouffer de ſes ondeux brouillars :
Mais où plus ce feu croiſt, plus elle diminue.
    Sui donc (mon cher ſouci) ce chemin non froyable
Que par ceux, que le ciel, liberal, veut benir,
Et ie iure qu en brief ie te feray tenir
Entre les bons eſprits quelque rang honorable.
    Ceſt par ce beau diſcours que la Muſe celeſte
Tenant vne couronne en ſa pucelle main,
Attire à ſoy mon cœur d vn tranſport plus qu'humain,
Tant bien à ſes doux mots elle adiouſte vn doux geſte.
    Depuis, ce ſeul amour dans mes veines bouillonne :
Depuis, ce ſeul vent ſoufle és toiles de ma nef :
Bien-heureux ſi ie puis non poſer ſur mon chef,
Ains du doigt ſeulement toucher ceſte couronne.

                F I N I S.

At one eare enters, and at the other goes.
Alas, I fe not one vnvaill his ene
From *Venus* vaill and gal prophane, that bene
To golden honnied verfe, the only harme,
Although our France with lofty fprits doth fwarme.
But thou my deir one, whome the holy *Nyne*,
Who yearly drinks *Pegafi*s fountaine fyne,
The great gods holy fongfter had receiued,
Yea, euen before thy mother the conceiued.
Albeit this fubieċt feame a barren ground,
With quickeft fpreits left ley, as they it found,
Irk not for that heirefter of thy paine,
Thy glore by rairnes greater fhall remaine.
O *Saluft*, lofe not heart, though pale Inuye
Bark at thy praife increafing to the fkye,
Feare not that fhe tread vnder foote thy verfe,
As if they were vnworthie to reherfe.
This monfter honnors-hurt is lyke the curr,
That barks at ftrangers comming to the durr,
But fparing alwaies thofe are to him knowin,
To them moft gentle, to the others throwin.
This monfter als is lyke a rauing cloude,
Which threatnes alwayis kendling *Vulcan* loude.
To fmore and drowne him, with her powring raine,
Yet force of fyre repellis her power againe.
Then follow furth, my fonne, that way unfeard,
Of them whom in fre heauens gift hath appeard.
And heare I fweare, thou fhortly fhall refaue
Some noble rank among good fpreits and graue.
This heauenly *Mufe* by fuch difcourfes fair,
Who in her Virgin hand a riche crowne bair:
So drew to her my heart, fo farr tranfported,
And with fwete grace, fo fwetely fhe exhorted:
As fince that loue into my braines did brew,
And fince that only wind my fhipfailles blew,
I thought me bleft, if I might only clame
To touche that crown, though not to weare the fame.

FINIS.

ANE METAPHORICALL

INVENTION OF A TRAGEDIE
CALLED PHOENIX.

A Colomne of 18 lynes feruing for a Preface
to the Tragedie enfuyng.

```
            ꞏ        Elf        1
               2   Echo   2
             3  help, that both  3
           4  together        we,  4
          .5  Since caufe there be, may  5
         6  now lament with tearis, My  6
        7  murnefull yearis.  Ye furies als  7
       8  with him, Euen Pluto grim, who duells  8
      9  in dark, that he, Since chief we fe him  9
     10  to you all that bearis The ftyle men fearis cf  10
   11  Diræ, I requeft, Eche greizlie gheft that dwells  11
  12  beneth the fee, With all yon thre, whofe hairs are fnaiks  12
  12  full blew, And all your crew, affift me in thir twa:  12
   11  Repeit and fha my Tragedie full neir, The  11
     10  chance fell heir. then fecundlie is beft, Deuills  10
       9  void of reft, ye moue all that it reid,  9
        8  With me in deid lyke dolour them  8
         7  to griv', I then will liv' in  7
          6  leffer greif therebj.  Kyth  6
           5  heir and try your force  5
            4  ay bent and quick,  4
             3  Excell      in  3
              2  fik  like  2
       1          ill,        1
              and murne with
           me.  From Delphos fyne
         Apollo cum with fpeid : Whofe  ꞏ
       fhining light my cairs will dim in deid.
```

✿ The expanſion of the
former Colomne.

E	·If Echo help, that both together w	E
(S	ince cauſe there be) may now lament with teari	S
M	y murneſull yearis. Ye furies als with hi	M
E	uen Pluto grim, who dwels in dark, that h	E
S	ince cheif we ſe him to you all that beari	S
T	he ſtyle men ſearis of Diræ : I requeſ	T
E	che greizlie gheſt, that dwells beneth the S	E
W	ith all yon thre, whoſe hairis ar ſnaiks full bJe	W
A	nd all your crew, aſſiſt me in thir tw	A
R	epeit and ſha my Tragedie full nei	R
T	he chance fell heir. Then ſecoundlie is beſ	T
D	euils void of reſt, ye moue all that it rei	D
W	ith me, indeid, lyke dolour thame to gri	·V
I	then will liv', in leſſer greif therebi	I
K	ythe heir and trie, your force ay bent and quic	K
E	xcell in ſik lyke ill, and murne with m	F.

From Delphos ſyne Apollo cum with ſpeid,
VVhoſe ſhining light my cairs wil dim in deid.

PHOENIX.

HE dyuers falls, that *Fortune* geuis
to men,
By turning ouer her quheill to their
annoy,
When I do heare them grudge,
although they ken
That old blind *Dame*, delytes to let
the ioy
Of all, fuche is her vfe, which dois conuoy
Her quheill by gefs : not looking to the right,
Bot ftill turnis vp that pairt quhilk is too light.

Thus quhen I hard fo many did complaine,
Some for the loffe of worldly wealth and geir,
Some death of frends, quho can not come againe :
Some loffe of health, which vnto all is deir,
Some loffe of fame, which ftill with it dois beir
Ane greif to them, who mereits it indeid :
Yet for all thir appearis there fome remeid.

For as to geir, lyke chance has made you want it,
Reftore you may the fame againe or mair.
For death of frends, although the fame (I grant it)
Can noght returne, yet men are not fo rair,
Bot ye may get the lyke.   For feiknes fair
Your health may come : or to ane better place
Ye muft.   For fame, good deids will mend difgrace.

Then, fra I faw (as I already told)
How men complaind for things whilk might amend,
How *Dauid Lindfay* did complaine of old
His *Papingo*, her death, and fudden end,
Ane common foule, whofe kinde be all is kend.
All thefe hes moved me prefently to tell
Ane Tragedie, in griefs thir to excell.

For I complaine not of fic common cace,
Which diuerfly by diuers means dois fall:
But I lament my *Phœnix* rare, whofe race,
Whofe kynde, whofe kin, whofe offspring, they be all
In her alone, whome I the *Phœnix* call.
That fowle which only one at onis did liue,
Not liues, alas! though I her praife reviue.

In *Arabie* cald *Fœlix* was fhe bredd
This foule, excelling *Iris* farr in hew.
Whofe body whole, with purpour was owercledd,
Whofe taill of coulour was celeftiall blew,
With fkarlat pennis that through it mixed grew:
Her craig was like the yallowe burnifht gold,
And fhe her felf thre hundreth yeare was old.

She might haue liued as long againe and mair,
If fortune had not ftayde dame *Naturs* will:
Six hundreth yeares and fourtie was her fcair,
Which *Nature* ordained her for to fulfill.
Her natiue foile fhe hanted euer ftill,
Except to *Egypt* whiles fhe tooke her courfe,
Wherethrough great *Nylus* down runs from his fourfe.

Like as ane hors, when he is barded haile,
An fethered pannach fet vpon his heid,
Will make him feame more braue: Or to affaile
The enemie, he that the troups dois leid,
Ane pannache on his healme will fet in deid:
Euen fo, had *Nature*, to decore her face;
Giuen her ane tap, for to augment her grace.

In quantitie, fhe dois refemble neare
Vnto the foule of mightie *Ioue*, by name
The *AEgle* calld : oft in the time of yeare,
She vfde to foir, and flie through diuers realme,
Out through the *Azure* fkyes, whill fhe did fhame
The Sunne himfelf, her coulour was fo bright,
Till he abafhit beholding fuch a light.

Thus whill fhe vfde to fcum the fkyes about,
At laft fhe chanced to fore out ower the fee
Calld *Mare Rubrum* : yet her courfe held out
Whill that fhe paft whole *Afie*. Syne to flie
To *Europe* fmall fhe did refolue : To drie
Her voyage out, at laft fhe came in end
Into this land, ane ftranger heir vnkend.

Ilk man did maruell at her forme moft rare
The winter came, and ftorms cled all the feild :
Which ftorms, the land of fruit and corne made bare,
Then did fhe flie into an houfe for beild,
VVhich from the ftorms might faue her as an fheild.
There, in that houfe fhe firft began to tame,
I came, fyne tooke her furth out of the fame.

Fra I her gat, yet none could gefs what fort
Of foule fhe was, nor from what countrey cum :
Nor I my felf : except that be her port,
And gliftring hewes I knew the fhe was fum
Rare ftranger foule, which oft had vfde to fcum
Through diuers lands, delyting in her flight ;
VVhich made vs fee, fo ftrange and rare a fight.

Whill at the laft, I chanced to call to minde
How that her nature, did refemble neir
To that of *Phœnix* which I red. Her kinde,
Her hewe, her fhape, did mak it plaine appeir,
She was the fame, which now was lighted heir.
This made me to efteme of her the more,
Her name and rarenes did her fo decore.

Thus being tamed, and throughly weill acquent.
She took delyte (as fhe was wount before)
VVhat tyme that *Titan* with his beames vpfprent,
To take her flight, amongs the fkyes to foire.
Then came to her of fowlis, a woundrous ftore
Of diuers kinds, fome fimple fowlis, fome ill
And rauening fowlis, whilks fimple onis did kill.

And euen as they do fwarme about their king
The hunnie *Bees*, that works into the hyue :
VVhen he delyts furth of the fkepps to fpring,
Then all the leaue will follow him belyue,
Syne to be nixt him biffelie they ftriue :
So, all thir fowlis did follow her with beir,
For loue of her, fowlis rauening did no deir.

Such was the loue, and reuerence they her bure,
Ilk day whill euen, ay whill they fhedd at night.
Fra time it darkned, I was euer fure
Of her returne, remaining whill the light,
And *Phœbus* ryfing with his garland bright.
Such was her trueth, fra time that fhe was tame,
She, who in brightnes *Titans* felf did fhame.

By vfe of this, and hanting it, at laft
She made the foules, fra time that I went out,
Aboue my head to flie, and follow faft
Her, who was chief and leader of the rout.
When it grew lait, fhe made them flie, but doubt,
Or feare, euen in the cloffe with her of will,
Syne fhe her felf, perkt in my chalmer ftill.

When as the countreys round about did heare
Of this her byding in this countrey cold,
Which not but hills, and darknes ay dois beare,
(And for this caufe was *Scotia* calld of old,)
Her lyking here, when it was to them told,
And how fhe greind not to go backe againe :
The loue they bure her, turnd into difdaine.

Lo, here the fruicts, whilks of *Inuy* dois breid,
To harme them all, who vertue dois imbrace.
Lo, here the fruicts, from her whilks dois proceid,
To harme them all, that be in better cace
Then others be. So followed they the trace
Of proud *Inuy*, thir countreyis lying neir,
That fuch a foule, fhould lyke to tary heir.

Whill Fortoun at the laft, not onely moued
Inuy to this, which could her not content,
Whill that *Inuy*, did feafe fom foules that loued
Her anis as femed : but yet their ill intent
Kythed, when they faw all other foules ftill bent
To follow her, mifknowing them at all.
This made them worke her vndeferued fall.

Thir were the rauening fowls, whome of I fpak
Before, the whilks (as I already fhew)
Was wount into her prefence to hald bak
Their crueltie, from fimples ones, that flew
With her, ay whill *Inuy* all feare withdrew.
Thir ware, the *Rauin*, the *Stainchell*, and the *Gled*,
With others kynds, whom in this malice bred.

Fra *Malice* thus was rooted be *Inuy*,
In them as fone the awin effects did fhaw.
VVhich made them fyne, vpon ane day, to fpy
And wait till that, as fhe was wount, fhe flaw
Athort the fkyes, fyne did they neir her draw,
Among the other fowlis of dyuers kynds,
Although they ware farr diffonant in mynds.

For where as they ware wount her to obey,
Their mynde farr contrair then did plaine appeare.
For then they made her as a commoun prey
To them, of whome fhe looked for no deare,
They ftrake at her fo bitterly, whill feare
Stayde other fowlis to preis for to defend her
From thir ingrate, whilks now had clene mifkend her.

When fhe could find none other faue refuge
From thefe their bitter ftraiks, fhe fled at laft
To me (as if fhe wolde wifhe me to iudge
The wrong they did her) yet they followed faft
Till fhe betuix my leggs her felfe did caft.
For fauing her from thefe, which her oppreft,
Whofe hote purfute, her fuffred not to reft.

Bot yet at all that ferved not for remeid,
For noghttheles, they fpaird her not a haire
In ftede of her, yea whyles they made to bleid
My leggs : (fo grew their malice mair and mair)
Which made her both to rage and to difpair,
Firft, that but caufe they did her fuch difhort :
Nixt, that fhe laked help in any fort.

Then hauing tane ane dry and wethered ftra,
In deip difpair, and in ane lofty rage
She fprang vp heigh, outfleing euery fa :
Syne to *Panchaia* came, to change her age
Vpon *Apollos* altar, to affwage
With outward fyre her inward raging fyre :
Which then was all her cheif and whole defyre.

Then being carefull, the event to know
Of her, who homeward had returnde againe
Where fhe was bred, where ftorms dois neuer blow,
Nor bitter blafts, nor winter fnows, nor raine,
But fommer ftill : that countray doeth fo ftaine
All realmes in fairnes.   There in hafte I fent,
Of her to know the yffew and event.

The meffinger went there into fic hafte,
As could permit the farrnes of the way,
By croffing ower fa mony countreys wafte
Or he come there.   Syne with a lytle ftay
Into that land, drew homeward euery day :
In his returne, lyke diligence he fhew
As in his going there, through realmes anew.

Fra he returnd, then fone without delay
I fpeared at him, (the certeantie to try)
What word of *Phœnix* which was flown away?
And if through all the lands he could her fpy,
Where through he went, I bad him not deny,
But tell the trueth, yea whither good or ill
Was come of her, to wit it was my will.

He tolde me then, how fhe flew bak againe,
Where fra fhe came, and als he did receit,
How in *Panchaia* toun, fhe did remaine
On *Phœbus* alter, there for to compleit
With *Thus* and *Myrrh*, and other odours fweit
Of flowers of dyuers kyndes, and of *Incens*
Her neft.   With that he left me in fufpens.

Till that I charged him no wayes for to fpair,
Bot prefently to tell me out the reft.
He tauld me then, How *Titans* garland thair
Inflamde be heate, reflexing on her neft,
The withered ftra, which when fhe was oppreft
Heir be yon fowlis, fhe bure ay whill fhe came
There, fyne aboue her neft fhe laid the fame.

And fyne he tolde, how fhe had fuch defyre
To burne her felf, as fhe fat downe therein.
Syne how the Sunne the withered ftra did fyre,
Which brunt her neft, her fethers, bones, and fkin
All turnd in afh.   Whofe end dois now begin
My woes : her death maks lyfe to greif in me.
She, whome I rew my eyes did euer fee.

O deuills of darknes, contraire vnto light,
In *Phœbus* fowle, how could ye get fuch place,
Since ye are hated ay be *Phœbus* bright?
For ftill is fene his light dois darknes chace.
But yet ye went into that fowle, whofe grace,
As *Phœbus* fowle, yet ward the Sunne him fell.
Her light his ftaind, whome in all light dois dwell.

And thou (ô *Phœnix*) why was thow fo moued
Thow foule of light, be enemies to thee,
For to forget thy heauenly hewes, whilkis loued
Were baith by men and fowlis that did them fee?
And fyne in hewe of afhe that they fould bee
Conuerted all : and that thy goodly fhape
In *Chaos* fould, and noght the fyre efcape?

And thow (ô reuthles *Death*) fould thow deuore
Her? who not only paffed by all mens mynde
All other fowlis in hew, and fhape, but more
In rarenes (fen there was none of her kynde
But fhe alone) whome with thy ftounds thow pynde :
And at the laft, hath perced her through the hart,
But reuth or pitie, with thy mortall dart.

Yet worft of all, fhe liued not half her age.
Why ftayde thou *Tyme* at leaft, which all dois teare
To worke with her? O what a cruel rage,
To cut her off, before her threid did weare !
VVherein all *Planets* keeps their courfe, that yeare
It was not by the half yet worne away,
Which fould with her haue ended on a day.

Then fra thir newis, in forrows foped haill,
Had made vs both a while to holde our peace,
Then he began and faid, Pairt of my taill
Is yet vntolde, Lo here one of her race,
Ane worm bred of her afhe : Though fhe, alace,
(Said he) be brunt, this lacks but plumes and breath
To be lyke her, new gendred by her death.

L'envoy.

Apollo then, who brunt with thy reflex
Thine onely fowle, through loue that thou her bure,
Although thy fowle, (whofe name doth end in X)
Thy burning heate on nowayes could indure,

D

But brunt thereby : Yet will I the procure,
Late foe to *Phœnix*, now her freind to be :
Reuiuing her by that which made her die.

Draw farr from heir, mount heigh vp through the air,
To gar thy heat and beames be law and neir.
That in this countrey, which is colde and bair,
Thy gliftring beames als ardent may appeir
As they were oft in *Arabie*: fo heir
Let them be now, to make ane *Phœnix* new
Euen of this worme of *Phœnix* afhe which grew.

This if thow dois, as fure I hope thou fhall,
My tragedie a comike end will haue :
Thy work thou hath begun, to end it all.
Els made ane worme, to make her out the laue.
This Epitaphe, then beis on *Phœnix* graue.
    Here lyeth, vvhome too euen be her death and end
    Apollo hath a longer lyfe her fend.

FINIS.

A PARAPHRASTICALL

TRANSLATION OVT OF
THE POETE LVCANE.

LVCANVS LIB.

QVINTO.

CAEfaris an curfus veftræ fentire putatis
Damnum poffe fugæ? Veluti fi cuncta minentur
Flumina, quos mifcent pelago, fubducere fontes :
Non magis ablatis vnquam decreuerit æquor,
Quam nunc crefcit aquis. An vos momenta putatis
Vlla dediffe mihi?

If all the floods amongft them wold conclude
To ftay their courfe from running in the fee :
And by that means wold thinke for to delude
The *Ocean*, who fould impaired be,
As they fuppofde, beleuing if that he
Did lack their floods, he fhould decreffe him felf :
Yet if we like the veritie to wye.
It pairs him nothing : as I fhall you tell.

For out of him they are augmented all,
And moſt part creat, as ye ſhall perſaue :
For when the Sunne doth ſouk the vapours ſmall
Forth of the ſeas, whilks them conteine and haue,
A part in winde, in wete and raine the laue
He render dois : which doth augment their ſtrands.
Of *Neptuns* woll a coate ſyne they him weaue,
By hurling to him faſt out ower the lands.

When all is done, do to him what they can   .
None can perſaue that they do ſwell him mair.
I put the caſe then that they neuer ran :
Yet not theleſs that could him nowiſe pair :
VVhat needs he then to count it, or to cair,
Except their folies wold the more be ſhawin ?
Sen though they ſtay, it harmes him not a hair,
What gain they, thogh they had their courſe withdrawen ?

So euen ſiclike : Though ſubieêts do coniure
For to rebell againſt their Prince and King :
By leauing him although they hope to ſmure
That grace, wherewith God maks him for to ring,
Though by his gifts he ſhaw him ſelfe bening,
To help their need, and make them thereby gaine :
Yet lack of them no harme to him doth bring,
VVhen they to rewe their folie ſhalbe faine.

L'enuoy.

Then *Floods* runne on your wounted courſe of olde,
Which God by Nature dewly hes prouyded :
For though ye ſtay, as I before haue tolde,
And caſt in doubt which God hath els decyded :
To be conioynde, by you to be deuyded :
To kythe your ſpite, and do the *Depe* no ſkaith :
Farre better were in others ilk confyded,
Ye *Floods*, thou *Depe*, whilks were your dewties baith.

F I N I S.

ANE SCHORT
TREATISE,

CONTEINING SOME REVLIS
and cautelis to be obseruit and
eschewit in Scottis
Poesie.

A QVADRAIN OF ALEXANDRIN
VERSE, DECLARING TO QVHOME THE
Authour hes directit his labour.

To ignorants obdurde, quhair vvilful errour lyis,
Nor zit to curious folks, quhilks carping dois. deiect thee,
Nor zit to learned men, quha thinks thame onelie vvyis,
Bot to the docile bairns of knavvledge I direct thee.

HE caufe why (docile Reader) I haue not dedicat this fhort treatife to any particular perfonis, (as commounly workis vfis to be) is, that I efteme all thais quha hes already fome beginning of knawledge, with ane earneft defyre to atteyne to farther, alyke meit for the reading of this worke, or any vther, quhilk may help thame to the atteining to thair foirfaid de-fyre. Bot as to this work, quhilk is intitulit, *The Reulis and cautelis to be obfcruit and efchevvit in Scottis Poefie*, ze may maruell paraventure, quhairfore I fould haue writtin in that mater, fen fa mony learnit men, baith of auld and of late hes already written thairof in dyuers and findry languages : I anfwer, That nocht-withftanding, I haue lykewayis writtin of it, for twa cauffis : The ane is, As for them that wrait of auld. lyke as the tyme is changeit fenfyne, fa is the ordour of Poefie changeit. For then they obferuit not *Flovving*, nor efchewit not *Ryming in termes*, befydes findrie vther thingis, quhilk now we obferue, and efchew, and dois weil in fa doing : becaufe that now, quhen the warld is waxit auld, we haue all their opinionis in writ, quhilk were learned before our tyme, befydes our awin ingynis, quhair as they then did it onelie be thair awin ingynis, but help of any vther. Thairfore, quhat I fpeik of Poefie now, I fpeik of it, as being come to mannis age and perfectioun, quhair as then, it was bot in the infancie and chyldheid. The vther caufe is, That as for thame that hes written in it of late, there hes neuer ane of thame written in our language. For albeit findrie hes written of it in Englifh, quhilk is lykeft to our language, zit we differ from thame in findrie reulis of Poefie, as ze will find be experience. I haue lyke-wayis omittit dyuers figures, quhilkis are neceffare to be vfit in verfe, for two caufis. The ane is, becaufe they are vfit in all languages, and thairfore are fpokin of be *Du Bellay*, and findrie vtheris, quha hes written

in this airt. Quhairfore gif I wrait of them alfo, it
fould feme that I did bot repete that, quhilk they
haue written, and zit not fa weil, as they haue done
already. The vther caufe is, that they are figures of
Rhetorique and Dialectique, quhilkis airtis I profeffe
nocht, and thairfore will apply to my felfe the counfale,
quhilk *Apelles* gaue to the fhoomaker, quhen he faid to
him, feing him find falt with the fhankis of the Image
of *Venus*, efter that he had found falt with the pantoun,
Ne futor vltra crepidam.

I will alfo wifh zow (docile Reidar) that or ze
cummer zow with reiding thir reulis, ze may find in
zour felf fic a beginning of Nature, as ze may put in
practife in zour verfe many of thir foirfaidis preceptis,
or euer ze fie them as they are heir fet doun. For gif
Nature be nocht the cheif worker in this airt, Reulis
wilbe bot a band to Nature, and will mak zow within
fhort fpace weary of the haill airt : quhair as, gif
Nature be cheif, and bent to it, reulis will be ane help
and ftaff to Nature. I will end heir, left my preface
be langer nor my purpofe and haill mater following :
wifhing zow, docile Reidar, als gude fucces and great
proffeit by reiding this fhort treatife, as I tuke earnift
and willing panis to blok it, as ze fie, for zour caufe.
Fare weill.

I Haue infert in the hinder end of this Treatife,
maift kyndis of verfis quhilks are not cuttit or
brokin, bot alyke many feit in euerie lyne of the verfe,
and how they are commounly namit, with my opinioun for
quhat fubiectis ilk kynde of thir verfe is meiteft to be vfit.

TO knaw the quantitie of zour lang or fhort fete in
they lynes, quhilk I haue put in the reule,
quhilk teachis zow to knaw quhat is *Flovving*, I haue
markit the lang fute with this mark,— and
abone the heid of the fhorte fute, I
haue put this mark ᴜ .

* *
*

SONNET OF THE AVTHOVR
TO THE READER.

Sen for zour ſaik I vvryte upon zour airt,
 Apollo, Pan, and ze ô Muſis nyne,
  And thou, ô Mercure, for to help thy pairt
I do implore, ſen thou be thy ingyne,
Nixt efter Pan had found the quhiſſill, ſyne
Thou did perfyte, that quhilk he bot eſpyit :
And efter that made Argus for to tyne
(quha kepit Io) all his vvindois by it.
Concurre ze Gods, it can not be denyit :
Sen in your airt of Poëſie I vvryte.
Auld birds to learne by teiching it is tryit :
Sic docens diſcans gif ze help to dyte.
 Then Reidar ſie of nature thou haue pairt,
 Syne laikis thou nocht, bot heir to reid the airt.

SONNET DECIFRING
THE PERFYTE POETE.

Ane rype ingyne, ane quick and vvalkned vvitt,
 VVith ſommair reaſons, ſuddenlie applyit,
  For euery purpoſe vſing reaſons fitt,
VVith ſkilfulnes, vvhere learning may be ſpyit,
With pithie vvordis, for to expres zovv by it
His full intention in his proper leid,
The puritie quhairof, vveill hes he tryit :
With memorie to keip quhat he dois reid,
With ſkilfulnes and figuris, quhilks proceid
From Rhetorique, vvith euerlaſting fame,
With vthers vvoundring, preaſſing vvith all ſpeid
For to atteine to merite ſic a name.
All thir into the perfyte Poëte be.
Goddis, grant I may obteine the Laurell trie.

THE REVLIS AND CAV-
TELIS TO BE OBSERVIT
and efchewit in Scottis
Poefie.

CAP. I

IRST, ze fall keip iuſt cullouris,
quhairof the cautelis are thir.

That ze ryme nocht twyfe in
ane fyllabe. As for exemple, that
ze make not *proue* and *reproue* ryme
together, nor *houe* for houeing on
hors bak, and *behoue.*

That ze ryme ay to the hinmeſt
lang fyllable, (with accent) in the lyne, fuppofe it be
not the hinmeſt fyllabe in the lyne, as *bakbyte zovv,*
and *out flyte zovv,* It rymes in *byte* and *flyte,* becaufe
of the lenth of the fyllabe, and accent being there, and
not in *zovv,* howbeit it be the hinmeſt fyllabe of
ather of the lynis. Or *queſtion* and *digeſtion,* It rymes
in *ques* and *ges,* albeit they be bot the antepenult
fyllabis, and vther twa behind ilkane of thame.

Ze aucht alwayis to note, That as in thir foirfaidis, or
the lyke wordis, it rymes in the hinmeſt lang fyllabe
in the lyne, althoucht there be vther ſhort fyllabis behind it, Sa is the hinmeſt lang fyllabe the hinmeſt
fute, fuppofe there be vther ſhort fyllabis behind it,
quhilkis are eatin vp in the pronounceing, and na wayis
comptit as fete.

Ze man be war likewayis (except necefsitie compell
yow) with *Ryming in Termis,* quhilk is to fay, that
your firſt or hinmeſt word in the lyne, exceid not twa
or thre fyllabis at the maiſt, vfing thrie als feindill as
ye can. The caufe quhairfore ze fall not place a lang
word firſt in the lyne, is, that all lang words hes ane

fyllabe in them fa verie lang, as the lenth thairof eatis
vp in the pronouncing euin the vther fyllabes, quhilks ar
placit lang in the fame word, and thairfore fpillis the
flowing of that lyne.   As for exemple, in this word,
Arabia, the fecond fyllable(*ra*) is fa lang, that it eatis
vp in the prononcing [*a*] quhilk is the hinmeſt fyllabe
of the fame word.   Quhilk [*a*] althocht it be in a lang
place, zit it kythis not fa, becaufe of the great lenth of
the preceding fyllable (*ra*).   As to the caufe quhy ze
fall not put a lang word hinmeſt in the lyne, It is, becaufe, that the lenth of the fecound fyllabe (*ra*) eating
vp the lenth of the vther lang fyllabe, [*a*] makis it to
ferue bot as a tayle vnto it, together with the ſhort
fyllabe preceding.   And becaufe this tayle nather feruis for cullour nor fute, as I fpak before, it man be
thairfore repetit in the nixt lyne ryming vnto it, as it
is fet doune in the firſt : quhilk makis, that ze will
fcarcely get many wordis to ryme vnto it, zea, nane at
all will ze finde to ryme to findrie vther langer wordis.
Thairfore cheifly be warre of inferting fic lang wordis
hinmeſt in the lyne, for the caufe quhilk I laſt allegit.
Befydis that nather firſt nor laſt in the lyne, it keipis
na *Flowring*.   The reulis and cautelis quhairof are
thir, as followis.

CHAP. II.

IRST, ze man vnderſtand that all fyllabis
are deuydit in thrie kindes : That is,
fome fchort, fome lang, and fome indifferent.   Be indifferent I meane, they quhilk
ere ather lang or ſhort, according as ze
place thame.

The forme of placeing fyllabes in verfe, is this.
That zour firſt fyllabe in the lyne be ſhort, the
fecond lang, the thrid ſhort, the fourt lang, the fyft
ſhort, the fixt lang, and fa furth to the end of the
lyne.   Alwayis tak heid, that the nomber of zour fete

in euery lyne be euin, and nocht odde : as four, fix, aucht, or ten : and not thrie, fyue, feuin, or nyne, except it be in broken verfe, quhilkis are out of reul and daylie inuentit be dyuers Poetis. Bot gif ze wald afk me the reulis, quhairby to knaw euerie ane of thir thre foirfaidis kyndis of fyllabes, I anfwer, Zour eare man be the onely iudge and difcerner thairof. And to proue this, I remit to the iudgement of the fame, quhilk of thir twa lynis following flowis beft,

$$\cup - \quad \cup \quad - \quad \cup \quad - \cup - \quad \cup \quad -$$

Into the Sea then Lucifer vpfprang.

$$\cup - \quad \cup \quad - \quad \cup - \cup \quad - \quad \cup \quad -$$

In the Sea then Lucifer to vfprang.

I doubt not bot zour eare makkis zou eafilie to perfaue, that the firft lyne flowis weil, and the vther nathing at all. The reafoun is, becaufe the firft lyne keips the reule abone written, to wit, the firft fute fhort, the fecound lang, and fa furth, as I fhewe before : quhair as the vther is direct contrair to the fame. Bot fpecially tak heid, quhen zour lyne is of fourtene, that zour *Sectioun* in aucht be a lang mono- fyllabe, or ellis the hinmeft fyllabe of a word alwais being lang, as I faid before. The caufe quhy it man be ane of thir twa, is, for the Mufique, becaufe that quhen zour lyne is ather of xiiij or xij fete, it wilbe drawin fa lang in the finging, as ze man reft in the middes of it, quhilk is the *Sectioun* : fa as, gif zour *Sectioun* be nocht ather a monofyllabe, or ellis the hinmeft fyllabe. of a word, as I faid before, bot the firft fyllabe of a polyfyllabe, the Mufique fall make zow fa to reft in the middes of that word, as it fall cut the ane half of the word fra the vther, and fa fall mak it feme twa different wordis, that is bot ane. This aucht onely to be obferuit in thir foirfaid lang lynis : for the fhortnes of all fhorter lynis, then thir before men- tionat, is the caufe, that the Mufique makis na reft in the middes of thame, and thairfore thir obferuationis feruis nocht for thame.   Onely tak heid, that the *Sectioun* in thame kythe fomething langer nor any vther feit in that lyne, except the fecound and the laft, as I haue faid before.

Ze man tak heid lykewayis, that zour langeft lynis exceid nochte fourtene fete, and that zour shorteft be nocht within foure.

Remember alfo to mak a *Sectioun* in the middes of euery lyne, quhether the lyne be lang or fhort.   Be *Sectioun* I mean, that gif zour lyne be of fourtene fete, zour aucht fute, man not only be langer then the feuint, or vther fhort fete, but alfo langer nor any vther lang fete in the fame lyne, except the fecound and the hinmeft.   Or gif your lyne be of twelf fete, zour *Sectioun* to be in the fext.   Or gif of ten, zour *Sectioun* to be in the fext alfo.   The caufe quhy it is not in fyue, is, becaufe fyue is odde, and euerie odde fute is fhort.   Or gif your lyne be of aucht fete, zour *Sectioun* to be in the fourt.   Gif of fex, in the fourt alfo.   Gif of four, zour *Sectioun* to be in twa.

Ze aucht likewife be war with oft compofing zour haill lynis of monofyllabis onely, (albeit our language haue fa many, as we can nocht weill efchewe it) becaufe the maift pairt of thame are indifferent, and may be in fhort or lang place, as ze like. _Some wordis of dyuers fyllabis are likewayis indifferent, as

Thairfore, reftore.

I thairfore, then.

In the firft, *thairfore,* (*thair*) is fhort, and *(fore)* is lang : In the vther, (*thair*) is lang, and *(fore)* is fhort, and zit baith flowis alike weill.   Bot thir indifferent wordis, compofit of dyuers fyllabes, are rare, fuppofe in monofyllabes, commoun.   The caufe then, quhy ane haill lyne aucht nocht to be compofit of mono-fyllabes only, is, that they being for the maift pairt indifferent, nather the fecound, hinmeft, nor *Sectioun*, will be langer nor the other lang fete in the fame lyne.

Thairfore ze man place a word compofit of dyuers fyllabes, and not indifferent, ather in the fecound, hinmeft, or *Sectioun*, or in all thrie.

Ze man alfo tak heid, that quhen thare fallis any fhort fyllabis efter the laft lang fyllabe in the lyne, that ze repeit thame in the lyne quhilk rymis to the vther, even as ze fet them downe in the firft lyne : as for exempill, ze man not fay

Then feir nocht
Nor heir ocht.

Bot
Then feir nocht
Nor heir nocht.

Repeting the fame, *nocht*, in baith the lynis : becaufe this fyllabe, *nocht*, nather feruing for cullour nor fute, is bot a tayle to the lang fute preceding, and thairfore is repetit lykewayis in the nixt lyne, quhilk rymes vnto it, euin as it fet doun in the firft.

There is alfo a kynde of indifferent wordis, afweill as of fyllabis, albeit few in nomber. The nature quhair-of is, that gif ze place thame in the begynning of a lyne, they are fhorter be a fute, nor they are, gif ze place thame hinmeft in the lyne, as

Sen patience I man haue perforce.
I liue in hope vvith patience.

Ze fe there are bot aucht fete in ather of baith thir lynis aboue written. The caufe quhairof is, that *patience*, in the firft lyne, in refpect it is in the be-ginning thairof, is bot of twa fete, and in the laft lyne, of thrie, in refpect it is the hinmeft word of that lyne. To knaw and difcerne thir kynde of wordis from vtheris, zour eare man be the onely iudge, as of all the vther parts of *Flovving*, the verie twicheftane quhair-of is Mufique.

I haue teachit zow now fhortly the reulis of *Ryming,*

Fete, and *Flow~ing*. There reftis yet to teache zow the wordis, fentences, and phrafis neceffair for a Poete to vfe in his verfe, quhilk I haue fet doun in reulis, as efter followis.

CHAP. III.

Irft, that in quhatfumeuer ze put in verfe, ze put in na wordis, ather *metri caufa*, or zit, for filling furth the nomber of the fete, bot that they be all fa neceffare, as ze fould be conftrainit to vfe thame, in cace ze were fpeiking the fame purpofe in profe. And thairfore that zour wordis appeare to haue cum out willingly, and by nature, and not to haue bene thrawin out conftrainedly, be compulfioun.

That ze efchew to infert in zour verfe, a lang rable of mennis names, or names of tounis, or fik vther names. Becaufe it is hard to mak many lang names all placit together, to flow weill. Thairfore quhen that fallis out in zour purpofe, ze fall ather put bot twa or thrie of thame in euerie lyne, mixing vther wordis amang thame, or ellis fpecifie bot twa or thre of them at all, faying (*With the laif of that race*) or (*With the rest in thay pairtis,*) or fic vther lyke wordis: as for example,

> *Out through his cairt, quhair Eous vvas eik*
> *VVith other thre, quhilk Phaëton had dravvin.*

Ze fie thair is bot ane name there fpecifeit, to ferue for vther thrie of that forte.

Ze man alfo take heid to frame zour wordis and fentencis according to the mater: As in Flyting and Inuectiues, zour wordis to be cuttit fhort, and hurland ouer heuch. For thais quhilkis are cuttit fhort, I meane be fic wordis as thir, *lis neir cair,*

for

I fall neuer cair, gif zour fubiect were of loue, or tragedies. Becaufe in thame zour words man be drawin lang, quhilkis in Flyting man be fhort.

Ze man lykewayis tak heid, the ze waill zour wordis according to the purpofe : As, in ane heich and learnit purpofe, to vfe heich, pithie, and learnit wordis.

Gif zour purpofe be of loue, To vfe commoun language, with fome paffionate wordis.

Gif zour purpofe be of tragicall materis, To vfe lamentable wordis, with fome heich, as rauifhit in admiratioun.

Gif zour purpofe be of landwart effairis, To vfe cor-ruptit and vplandis wordis.

And finally, quhatfumeuer be zour fubiect, to vfe *vocabula artis,* quhairby ze may the mair viuelie reprefent that perfoun, quhais pairt ze paint out.

This is likewayis neidfull to be vfit in fentences, als weill as in wordis. As gif zour fubiect be heich and learnit, to vfe learnit and infallible reafonis, prouin be neceffities.

Gif zour fubiect be of loue, To vfe wilfull reafonis, proceding rather from paffioun, nor reafoun.

Gif zour fubiect be of landwart effaris, To vfe fklender reafonis, mixt with groffe ignorance, nather keiping forme nor ordour. And fa furth, euer framing zour reafonis, according to the qualitie of zour fubiect.

Let all zour verfe be *Literall,* fa far as may be, quhatfumeuer kynde they be of, bot fpeciallie *Tumbling* verfe for flyting. Be *Literall* I meane, that the maift pairt of zour lyne, fall rynne vpon a letter, as this tumbling lyne rynnis vpon F.

Fetching fude for to feid it faft furth of the Farie.

Ze man obferue that thir *Tumbling* verfe flowis not on that faffoun, as vtheris dois. For all vtheris keipis the reule quhilk I gaue before, To wit, the firft fute fhort the fecound lang, and fa furth. Quhair as thir

hes twa fhort, and ane lang throuch all the lyne, quhen
they keip ordour : albeit the maift pairt of thame be
out of ordour, and keipis na kynde nor reule of *Flovving*,
and for that caufe are callit *Tumbling* verfe : except
the fhort lynis of aucht in the hinder end of the verfe,
the quhilk flowis as vther verfes dois, as ze will find in
the hinder end of this buke, quhair I gaue exemple of
findrie kyndis of verfis.

CHAP. IIII.

ARK alfo thrie fpeciall ornamentis to verfe,
quhilkis are, *Comparifons, Epithetis,* and
Prouerbis.

As for *Comparifons,* take heid that they
be fa proper for the fubiect, that nather
they be ouer bas, gif zour fubiect be heich, for then
fould zour fubiect [*Comparifoun* ?] difgrace zour *Comparifoun* [fubject ?], nather zour *Comparifoun* be heich
quhen zour fubiect is baffe, for then fall zour *Comparifoun* [fubject ?] difgrace your fubiect [*Comparifoun* ?].
Bot let fic a mutuall correfpondence and fimilitude be
betwix them, as it may appeare to be a meit *Comparifoun* for fic a fubiect, and fa fall they ilkane decore
vther.

As for *Epithetis,* It is to defcryue brieflie, *en paffant,*
the naturall of euerie thing ze fpeik of, be adding the
proper adiectiue vnto it, quhairof there are twa faffons.
The ane is, to defcryue it, be making, a corruptit worde,
compofit of twa dyuers fimple wordis, as

Apollo gyde-Sunne

The vther faffon, is, be *Circumlocution,* as

Apollo reular of the Sunne.

I efteme this laft faffoun beft, Becaufe it expreffis
the authoris meaning als weill as the vther, and zit
makis na corruptit wordis, as the vther dois.

As for the *Prouerbis,* they man be proper for the
fubiect, to beautifie it, chofen in the fame forme as the
Comparifoun.

CHAP V.

T is alſo meit, for the better decoratioun of the verſe to vſe ſumtyme the figure of Repetitioun, as

> *Quhylis ioy rang,*
> *Quhylis noy rang. &c.*

Ze ſie this word *quhylis* is repetit heir. This forme of repetitioun ſometyme vſit, decoris the verſe very mekle. zea quhen it cummis to purpoſe, it will be cumly to repete ſic a word aucht or nyne tymes in a verſe.

CHAP. VI.

ZE man alſo be warre with compoſing ony thing in the ſame maner, as hes bene ower oft vſit of before. As in ſpeciall, gif ze ſpeik of loue, be warre ze deſcryue zour *Loues* makdome, or her fairnes. And ſiclyke that ze deſcryue not the morning, and ryſing of the Sunne, in the Preface of zour verſe: for thir thingis are ſa oft and dyuerſlie writtin vpon be Poëtis already, that gif ze do the lyke, it will appeare, ze bot imitate, and that it cummis not of zour awin *Inuentioun*, quhilk is ane of the cheif properteis of ane Poete. Thairfore gif zour ſubiect be to prayſe zour *Loue*, ze ſall rather prayſe hir vther qualiteis, nor her fairnes, or hir ſhaip : or ellis ze ſall ſpeik ſome lytill thing of it, and ſyne ſay, that zour wittis are ſa ſmal, and zour vtterance ſa barren, that ze can not diſcryue any part of hir worthelie : remitting alwayis to the Reider, to iudge of hir, in reſpect ſho matches, or rather excellis *Venus*, or any woman, quhome to it ſall pleaſe zow to compaire her. Bot gif zour ſubiect be ſic, as ze man ſpeik ſome thing of the morning, or Sunne ryſing, tak heid, that quhat name ze giue to the Sunne, the Mone, or vther ſtarris, the ane tyme, gif ze happin to wryte

E

thairof another tyme, to change thair names.   As gif ze
call the Sunne *Titan*, at a tyme, to call him *Phœbus* or
Apollo the vther tyme, and ficlyke the Mone, and vther
Planettis.

CHAP. VII.

OT fen *Inuention*, is ane of the cheif vertewis
in a Poete, it is beft that ze inuent zour
awin fubiect, zour felf, and not to com-
pofe of fene fubiectis.   Efpecially, tranflating any thing out of vther language, quhilk
doing, ze not onely effay not zour awin ingyne of *Inuentioun*, bot be the fame meanes, ze are bound, as to a
ftaik, to follow that buikis phrafis, quhilk ze tranflate.

Ze man alfo be war of wryting any thing of materis
of commoun weill, or vther fic graue fene fubiectis
(except Metaphorically, of manifeft treuth opinly
knawin, zit nochtwithftanding vfing it very feindil) becaufe nocht onely ze effay nocht zour awin *Inuentioun*,
as I fpak before, bot lykewayis they are to graue
materis, for a Poet to mell in.   Bot becaufe ze can not
haue the *Inuentioun*, except it come of Nature, I remit
it thairvnto, as the cheif caufe, not onely of *Inuentioun*,
bot alfo of all the vther pairtis of Poefie.   For airt is
onely bot ane help and a remembraunce to Nature, as
I fhewe zow in the Preface.

CHAP. VIII. tuiching the kyndis of verfis,
mentionat in the Preface.

Irft, there is ryme quhilk feruis onely for
lang hiftoreis, and zit are nocht verfe As
for exemple,

In Maii vvhenthatthebliffefull Phœbusbricht,
The lamp of ioy, the heauens gemme of licht,
The goldin cairt, and the etheriall King,
With purpour face in Orient dois fpring,
Maift angel-lyke afcending in his fphere,
And birds vvith all thair heauenlie voces cleare

Dois mak a fvveit and heauinly harmony,
And fragrant flours dois spring vp lustely :
Into this seafon fvveitest of delyte,
To vvalk I had a lusty appetyte.

And fa furth.

¶ For the defcriptioun of Heroique actis, Martiall and knichtly faittis of armes, vfe this kynde of verfe following, callit *Heroicall*, As

Meik mundane mirrour, myrrie and modest,
Blyth, kynde, and courtes, comelie, clene, and chest,
To all exemple for thy honeftie,
As richest rofe, or rubic, by the rest,
VVith gracis graue, and gesture maist digest,
Ay to thy honnour alvvayis hauing eye.
Were fafsons fiiemde, they micht be found in the :
Of blissings all, be blyth, thovv hes the best,
VVith euerie berne belouit for to be.

¶ For any heich and graue fubiectis, fpecially drawin out of learnit authouris, vfe this kynde of verfe following, callit *Ballat Royal*, as

That nicht he ceift, and vvent to bed, bot greind
Zit faft for day, and thocht the nicht to lang :
At laft Diana doun her head recleind,
Into the fea.   Then Lucifer vpfprang,
Auroras post, vvhome fho did fend amang
The Ieittie cludds, for to foretell ane hour,
Before fho ftay her tears, quhilk Ouide fang
Fell for her loue, quhilk turnit in a flour.

¶ For tragicall materis, complaintis, or teftamentis, vfe this kynde of verfe following, callit *Troilus* verfe, as

To thee Echo, and thovv to me agane,
In the defert, amangs the vvods and vvells,
Quhair deftinie hes bound the to remane,
But company, vvithin the firths and fells,
Let vs complein, vvith vvofull zoutts and zells,

A ſhaft, a ſhotter, that our harts hes ſlane :
To thee Echo, and thovv to me agane.

¶ For flyting, or Inuectiues, vſe this kynde of verſe
following, callit *Rouncefallis*, or *Tumbling* verſe.

In the hinder end of haruest vpon Alhallovv ene,
Quhen our gude nichtbors rydis (nou gif I reid richt)
Some bucklit on a benvvod, and ſome on a bene,
Ay troll and into troupes fra the tvvylicht :
Some ſadland a ſho ape, all grathed into grene :
Some hotche and on a hemp ſtalk, hovand on a heicht.
The king of Fary vvith the Court of the Elf quene,
VVith many elrage Incubus rydand that nicht :
    There ane elf on ane ape ane vnſell begat :
    Beſyde a pot baith auld and vvorne,
    This bratshard in ane bus vvas borne :
    They ſand a monſter on the morne,
        VVar facit nor a Cat.

¶ For compendious prayſing of any bukes, or the
authouris thairof, or ony argumentis of vther hiſtoreis.
quhair ſundrie ſentences, and change of purpoſis are
requyrit, vſe *Sonet* verſe, of ſourtene lynis, and ten ſete
in euery lyne. The exemple quhairof, I neid nocht
to ſhaw zow, in reſpect I haue ſet doun twa in the be-
ginning of this treatiſe.

¶ In materis of loue, vſe this kynde of verſe, quhilk
we call *Commoun* verſe, as

    Quhais anſvver made thame nocht ſa glaid
    That they ſould thus the victors be,
    As euen the anſvver quhilk I haid
    Did greatly ioy aud confort me :
    Quhen lo, this ſpak Apollo myne,
    All that thou ſeikis, it ſall be thyne.

¶ Lyke verſe of ten ſete, as this foirſaid is of aucht, ze
may vſe lykewayis in loue materis : as alſo all kyndis
of cuttit and brokin verſe, quhairof new formes are
daylie inuentit according to the Poëtes pleaſour, as

Quha vvald haue tyrde to heir that tone,
Quhilk birds corroborat ay abone
   Throuch schouting of the Larkis?
They sprang sa heich into the skyes
Quhill Cupide vvalknis vvith the cryis
   Of Naturis chapell Clarkis.
Then leauing all the Heauins aboue
   He lichted on the eard.
Lo! hovv that lytill God of loue.
   Before me then appeard,
So myld-lyke
          VVith bovv thre quarters skant
And chyld-lyke

   So moylie
         He lukit lyke a Sant.
   And coylie

And sa furth.

¶ This onely kynde of brokin verse abonewrittin, man of necessitie, in thir last short fete, as *so moylie and coylie*, haue bot twa fete and a tayle to ilkane of thame, as ze sie, to gar the cullour and ryme be in the penult syllabe.

¶ And of thir foirsaidis kyndes of ballatis of haill verse, and not cuttit or brokin as this last is, gif ze lyke to put ane owerword till ony of thame, as making the last lyne of the first verse, to be the last lyne of euerie vther verse in that ballat, will set weill for loue materis. Bot besydis thir kyndes of brokin or cuttit verse, quhilks ar inuentit daylie be Poetis, as I shewe before, there are sindrie kyndes of haill verse, with all thair lynis
alyke lang, quhilk I haue heir omittit, and tane bot
onelie thir few kyndes abone specifeit
as the best, quhilk may be applyit to ony kynde of
subiect,
bot rather to thir, quhairof
I haue spokin before.

       ❉ ❉ ❉
         ❉

THE CIIII. PSALME,

TRANSLATED OVT OF

TREMELLIVS.

PSALME CIIII.

O Lord infpyre my fpreit and pen, to praife
Thy Name, whofe greatnes farr furpaffis all :
That fyne, I may thy gloir and honour blaife,
Which cleithis the ouer : about the lyke a wall
The light remainis.   O thow, whofe charge and call
Made Heauens lyke courtenis for to fpred abreid,
Who bowed the waters fo, as ferue they fhall
For criftall fyilring ouer thy houfe to gleid.

Who walks vpon the wings of reftles winde,
Who of the clouds his chariot made, euen he,
Who in his prefence ftill the fpreits doeth find,
Ay ready to fulfill ilk iuft decrie
Of his, whofe feruants fyre and flammis they be.
Who fet the earth on her fundations fure,
So as her brangling none fhall euer fee :
Who at thy charge the deip vpon her bure.

So, as the very tops of mountains hie
Be fluidis were onis ouerflowed at thy command,
Ay whill thy thundring voice fone made them flie
Ower hiddeous hills and howes, till noght but fand
Was left behind, fyne with thy mightie hand
Thow limits made vnto the roring deip.
So fhall fhe neuer droun againe the land,
But brek her wawes on rockis, her mairch to keip.

Thir are thy workis, who maid the ftrands to breid,
Syne rinn among the hills from fountains cleir,

Whairto wyld Affes oft dois rinn with fpeid,
With vther beafts to drinke.   Hard by we heir
The chirping birds among the leaues, with beir
To fing, whil all the rocks about rebounde.
A woundrous worke, that thow, ô Father deir,
Maks throtts fo fmall yeild furth fo greate a founde !

O thow who from thy palace oft letts fall
(For to refrefh the hills) thy bleffed raine :
Who with thy works mainteins the earth and all :
Who maks to grow the herbs and grafs to gaine.
The herbs for foode to man, grafs dois remaine
For food to horfe, and cattell of all kynde.
Thow caufeft them not pull at it in vaine,
But be thair foode. fuch is thy will and mynde.

Who dois reioyfe the hart of man with wyne,
And who with oyle his face maks cleir and bright,
And who with foode his ftomack ftrengthnes fyne,
Who nurifhes the very treis aright.
The *Cedars* evin of *Liban* tall and wight
He planted hath, where birds do bigg their neft.
He maid the *Firr* treis of a woundrous hight,
Where *Storks* dois mak thair dwelling place, and reft.

Thow made the barren hills, wylde goats refuge.
Thow maid the rocks, a refidence and reft
For *Alpin* ratts, where they doe liue and ludge.
Thow maid the *Moone*, her courfe, as thou thoght beft.
Thow maid the *Sûnne* in tyme go to, that left
He ftill fould fhyne, then night fould neuer come.
But thow in ordour all things hes fo dreft,
Some beafts for day, for night are alfo fome.

For Lyons young at night beginnis to raire,
And from their denns to craue of God fome pray :
Then in the morning, gone is all their caire,
And homeward to their caues rinnis faft, fra day
Beginne to kythe, the Sunne dois fo them fray.

Then man gois furth, fra tyme the Sunne dois ryfe.
And whill the euening he remanis away
At lefume labour, where his liuing lyes.

How large and mightie are thy workis, ô Lord!
And with what wifedome are they wrought, but faile.
The earths great fulnes, of thy gifts recorde
Dois beare: Heirof the Seas (which dyuers fkaile
Of fifh contenis) dois witnes beare: Ilk faile
Of dyuers fhips vpon the fwolling wawes
Dois teftifie, as dois the monftrous whaile,
Who frayis all fifhes with his ravening Iawes.

All thir (ô Lord) yea all this woundrous heape
Of liuing things, in feafon craues their fill
Of foode from thee. Thow giuing, Lord, they reape:
Thy open hand with gude things fills them ftill
When fo thow lift: but contrar, when thow will
Withdraw thy face, then are they troubled fair,
Their breath by thee receavd, fone dois them kill:
Syne they returne into their afhes bair.

But notwithftanding, Father deare, in cace
Thow breath on them againe, then they reviue.
In fhort, thow dois, ô Lord, renewe the face
Of all the earth, and all that in it liue.
Therefore immortall praife to him we giue:
Let him reioyfe into his works he maid,
Whofe looke and touche, fo hills and earth dois greiue.
As earth dois tremble, mountains reikis, afraid.

To *Iehoua* I all my lyfe fhall fing,
To found his Name I euer ftill fhall cair:
It fhall be fweit my thinking on that King:
In him I fhall be glaid for euer mair:
O let the wicked be into no whair
In earth.   O let the finfull be deftroyde.
Bleffe him my foule who name *Iehoua* bair:
O bleffe him now with notts that are enioydc.
                              Hallclu-iah.

ANE SCHORT POEME
OF TYME.

* * *
*

AS I was panfing in a morning, aire,
  And could not fleip, nor nawayis take me reft,
  Furth for to walk, the morning was fa faire,
Athort the feilds, it femed to me the beft.
The *Eaft* was cleare, whereby belyue I geft
That fyrie *Titan* cumming was in fight,
Obfcuring chaft *Diana* by his light.

VVho by his ryfing in the *Azure* fkyes,
Did dewlie helfe all thame on earth do dwell.
The balmie dew through birning drouth he dryis,
VVhich made the foile to fauour fweit and fmell,
By dewe that on the night before downe fell,
·VVhich then was foukit by the *Delphienns* heit
Vp in the aire : it was fo light and weit.

Whofe hie afcending in his purpour Sphere
Prouoked all from *Morpheus* to flee :
As beafts to feid, and birds to fing with beir,
Men to their labour, biffie as the Bee :
Yet ydle men deuyfing did I fee.
How for to dryue the tyme that did them irk,
By findrie paftvmes, quhill that it grew mirk.

Then woundred I to fee them feik a wyle,
So willinglie the precious tyme to tyne:
And how they did them felfis fo farr begyle,
To fafhe of tyme, which of it felfe is fyne.
Fra tyme be paft, to call it bakwart fyne
Is bot in vaine: therefore men fould be warr,
To fleuth the tyme that flees fra them fo farr.

For what hath man bot tyme into this lyfe,
Which giues him dayis his God aright to knaw:
Wherefore then fould we be at fic a ftryfe,
So fpedelie our felfis for to withdraw
Euin from the tyme, which is on nowayes flaw
To flie from vs, fuppofe we fled it noght?
More wyfe we were, if we the tyme had foght.

Bot fen that tyme is fic a precious thing,
I wald·we fould beftow it into that
Which were moft pleafour to our heauenly King.
Flee ydilteth, which is the greateft lat.
Bot fen that death to all is deftinat,
Let vs imploy that time that God hath fend vs,
In doing weill, that good men may commend vs.

Hæc quoque perficiat, quod perficit omnia, Tempus.

FINIS.

A TABLE OF SOME OBSCVRE
WORDIS WITH THEIR SIG-
nifications, efter the ordour of
the Alphabet.

* *
*

VVordis	Significations
Ammon	Iupiter Ammon.
Ande	A village befyde *Mantua* where *Virgill* was borne.
Alexandria	A famous citie in *Egypt*, where was the notable librarie gathered by *Ptolomeus Philadelphus*.

B

Bethaniens fecond liuing   *Lazarus* of *Bethania*, who was reuiued be Chrift, reid *Iohn* 11 Chap.

C

Castalia	A well at the fute of the hill *Parnaffus*.
Celæno	The cheif of the *Harpyes*, a kynde of monfters with wingis and womens faces, whome the Poets feynzeis to reprefent theuis.
Cerberus	The thrie headed porter of hell.
Cimmerien night	Drevin from a kynd of people in the Eaft, called *Cimmerij*, who are great theuis, and dwellis in dark caues, and therefore, fleeping in finne, is called *Cimmerien* night.
Circuler daunce	The round motionis of the Planets, and of their heauens, applyed to feuin findrie metallis.
Clio	One of the *Mufes*.
Cypris	The dwelling place of *Venus*, tearming *continens pro contento*.
Cyprian torche	Iouis darte.

D

Delphien Songs   Poemes, and verfes, drawen from the Oracle of *Apollo* at *Delphos.*

Diræ   Thre furies of hell, *Alecto, Megera,* and *Tefiphone.*

Dodon   A citie of the kingdome of *Epirus,* befydes the which, there was a wood and a Temple therein, confecrated to *Iupiter.*

E

Electre   A metal, fowre parts gold and fift part filuer.

Elife field   In Latin *Campi Elifij,* a ioy full place in hell, where as the Poets feinzeis all the happie fpreits do remaine.

Efculape   A mediciner, after made a god.

G

Greateft thunders   *Iupiter* (as the Poets feinzeis) had two thunders, whereof he fent the greateft vpon the Gyants, who contemned him.

H

(*Hermes*)   An AEgiptian *Philofopher* foone after the tyme of *Moyfes,* confeffed in his Dialogues one onely God to be Creator of all things, and graunted the errours of his forefathers, who brought in the fuperftitious worfhipping of Idoles.

Hippolyte   After his members were drawin in funder by fowre horfes, *Efculapius* at *Neptuns* requeft, glewed them together, and reuiued him.

M

Maufole tombe   One of the feauin miracles which *Artemife* caufed to be builded for her hufband by *Timotheus, Briace, Scope,* and fundrie other workmen.

Mein   A riuer in *Almanie*.
Sein   A riuer in *Fraunce*.
  The Authors meaning of thefe two riuers is, that the originall of the *Almanis* came firft out of *Fraunce*, contrarie to the vulgar opinion.

N

Nynevoiced mouth   The nyne *Mufes*, whereof *Vranie* was one.

P

Panchaia   A towne in the Eaft, wherein, it is written, the *Phœnix* burnis her felfe vpon *Apollos* altar.
Pinde or *Pindus*   A hill confecrate to *Apollo*, and the *Mufes*.
Phœmonoe   A woman who pronounced the Oracles of *Apollo*.

S

Seamans ftarres   The feauen ftarres.
Semele   Mother of *Bacchus*, who being deceiued by *Iuno*, made *Iupiter* come to her in his leaft thunder, which neuerthelefs confumde her.
Syrenes   Taken heir for littill gray birdes of *Canaria*.

T

Thais   A common harlot of *Alexandria*.
Triton   A monfter in the fea, fhapen like a man.
Turnus fifter   Named *Iuturna*, a goddefse of the water, who in the fhape of her brothers waggonner led his chariot through the fields, ay till *Alecto* appeared vnto them in the fhape of an Howlet.

V

Vranie   The heauenly Mufe.

FINIS.

Sonnet of the Authour.

THE facound Greke, *Demoſthenes* by name,
   His toung was ones into his youth ſo ſlow,
   As evin that airt, which flooriſh made his fame,
He ſcarce could name it for a tyme, ze know.   Rhetorique.
So of ſmall ſeidis the *Liban* Cedres grow :
So of an Egg the *Egle* doeth proceid :
From fountains ſmall great *Nilus* flood doeth flow :
Evin ſo of rawnis do mightie fiſhes breid.
Therefore, good Reader, when as thow dois reid
Theſe my firſt fruictis, diſpyſe them not at all.
Who watts, both theſe may able be indeid
Of fyner Poemis the begynning ſmall.
   Then, rather loaue my meaning and my panis,
   Then lak my dull ingyne and blunted branis.

FINIS.

I HAVE INSERT FOR
THE FILLING OVT OF THIR
VACAND PAGEIS, THE VERIE
wordis of *Plinius* vpon the

Phœnix,

as followis

* * *
*

C. PLINII
Nat. Hiſt. Lib. Decimi, Cap. 2.
De Phœnice.

* *
*

Ethiopes atque Indi, diſcolores maximè et inenarrabiles ferunt aues, et ante omnes nobilem Arabia Phœnicem: haud ſcio an fabulosè, vnum in toto orbe, nec viſum magnopere. Aquilæ narratur magnitudine, auri fulgore circa colla, cætera purpureus, cœruleam roſeis caudam pennis diſtinguentibus, criſtis faciem, capútque plumeo apice cohoneſtante. Primus atque diligentiſſimus togatorum de eo prodidit Manilius, Senator ille, maximis nobilis doctrinis doctore nullo: neminem extitiſſe qui viderit veſcentem: ſacrum in Arabia Soli eſſe, viuere annis DCLX. ſeneſcentem, caſia thuriſque ſurculis conſtruere nidum, replere odoribus, et ſuperemori. Ex oſſibus deinde et memedullis eius naſci primo ceuvermiculum: inde fieri pullum; principióque iuſta funeri priori reddere, et totum deferre nidum prope Panchaiam in Solis vrbem, et in ara ibi deponere. Cum huius alitis vita magni conuer-

üonem ann fieri prodit idem Manilius, iterumque ſig-
nificationes tempeſtatum et ſiderum eaſdem reuerti.
Hoc autem circa meridiem incipere, quo die ſignum
Arietis Sol intrauerit. Et fuiſſe eius conuerſionis
annum prodente ſe P. Licinio, M. Cornelio Conſul-
ibus. Cornelius Valerianus Phœnicem deuolaſſe in
AEgyptum tradit, Q. Plautio, Sex. Papinio Coss. Alla-
tus eſt et in vrbem Claudij Principis Cenſura, anno
vrbis DCCC, et in comitio propoſitus, quod actis
teſtatum eſt, ſed quem falſum eſſe nemo dubitaret.

FINIS.

*I helped my ſelf alſo in my Tragedie thairof, with
the Phœnix of Lactantius Firmianus, with
Geſnerus de Auibus, and dyuers vthers,
bot I haue onely inſert thir foreſaid words of Plinius,
Becauſe I follow
him maiſt in
my Tra-
gedie.
Farewell.*

On the Introduction and Early use of Tobacco in England.

For a difcuffion as to the knowledge and ufe of Tobacco previous to the Difcovery of America : fee *The Athenæum* for 27 June and 1 Auguft 1857.

I. **1577.** The earlieft detailed account of the herb Tobacco in the Englifh language I believe to be, "*Joyfull newes oute of the newe founde worlde* . . . Englifhed by JOHN FRAMPTON Marchant." London. 1577. A work reprinted in 1580, 1596, &c.

In his Dedication—dated London, 1 Oct. 1577—to 'Mafter Edwarde Dier Efquire,' Frampton informs us :

Retourning right worshipfull, home into Englande oute of Spaine, and novv not pressed vvith the former toiles of my old trade, I to passe the tyme to some benefite of my countrie, and to auoyde idlenesse : touke in hande to translate out of Spanishe into Englishe, the thre bookes of Doctour Monardes of Seuill, the learned Phisition, treatyng of the singuler and rare vertues of certaine Hearbes, Trees, Oyles, Plantes, Stones, and Drugges of the Weste Indies . . . .

NICHOLAS MONARDES had firft publifhed his account of Tobacco in the Second Part of his *De las Cofas que traen de neuftras Indias Occidentales que firuen en medicina.* Publifhed at Seville in 1571, and republifhed there, all three parts together, in 1574.

The following extracts are taken from the fecond edition of *Joyfull newes,* 1580 : which Frampton defcribes as "Newly corrected as by conference with the olde copies may appeare." Monardes tells us—

This Hearbe which commonly is called *Tabaco*, is an Hearbe of much antiquitie, and knowen amongst the Indians, and in especially among them of the new Spayne, and after that those Countries were gotten by our Spaniardes, beyng taught of the Indians, they did profite themselues with those things, in the wounds which they receiued in their Warres, healing themselues therewith to the great benefite.

Within these few yeeres [Monardes is writing in 1571] there hath beene brought into Spayne of it, more to adornate Gardens with the fairnesse thereof, and to geue a pleasant sight, than that it was thought to haue the maruellous medicinable vertues, which it hath, but nowe wee doe vse it more for his vertues. than for his fairenesse. For surely they are such which doe bring admiration. . . .

The proper name of it amongest the Indians is *Picielt,* for the name of *Tabaco* is geuen to it by our Spainardes, by reason of an Islande that is named *Tabaco.* . . .

: One of the meruelles of this Hearbe, and that which bringeth most admiration, is, the maner howe the Priestes of the Indias did vse it, which was in this manner : when there was emongest the Indians any manner of businesse, of greate importaunce, in the which the chiefe gentlemen called *Casiques*,or any of the principall people of the countrie, had necessitie to consult with their Priestes, in any businesse of importance ; they went and propounded their matter to their chiefe Priest, forthwith in their presence, he tooke certaine leaues of the *Tabaco,* and cast them into the fire, and did receiue the smoke of them at his mouth, and at his nose with a Cane,

F

and in taking of it, hee fell downe vppon the ground, as a Dead man, and remayning so, according to the quantitie of the smoke that he had taken, and when the hearbe had done his worke, he did reuiue and awake, and gaue them their answeres, according to the visions, and illusions which hee sawe, whiles he was rapte in the same manner, and he did interprete to them, as to him seemed best, or as the Deuill had counselled him, geuing them continual'y d ubtfull answeares, in such sorte, that howsoeuer it fell out, they might say that it was the same, which was declared, and the answeare that he made.

In like sort the rest of the Indians for their pastime, doe take the smoke of the *Tabaco*, too make themselues drunke withall, and to see the visions, and thinges that represent vnto them that wherein they doe delight: and other times thy take it to knowe their businesse, and successe, because conformable to that, whiche they haue seene beyng drunke therewith, euen so they iudge of their businesse. And as the Deuil is a deceauer, and hath the knowledge of the vertue of hearbes, so he did shew the vertue of this Hearb, that by the meanes thereof, they might see their imaginations, and visions, that he hath represented to them, and by that meanes deceiue them.

So far Monardes. The page following his account begins thus :—

Hereafter followeth a further addition of the Hearbe called Tabaco, otherwise called by the Frenchmen *Nicotiane*. Which hearbe hath done great cures in the Realme of *Fraunce* and *Portugal*, as heereafter at large may appeare in this treatise following.

This treatise is not found in Monardes : but was taken by Frampton from a celebrated French author.

After the death of CHARLES ESTIENNE, another French doctor, JOHN LIEBAUT, edited successiue editions of his *L'Agriculture, et Maifen Ruftique*, in 1564, 1565, 1570, 1574, &c. : until the names of the two medical men became identified with this popular work.

In the edition of 1570, at *p.* 79, b. ii. c. 76, will be found the French text of 'the treatise following,' which Frampton slipped into a totally different author. Of this treatise, we shall give the essential portions, becaufe it contains Nicot's own account of the introduction of Tobacco into France, within the decade preceding his relation.

Liébault thus begins his difcourfe :—

Nicotiane, although it bee not long since it hath beene knowne in France, notwithstanding deserueth palme and price, and among al other medicinable hearbs, it deserueth to stand in the first rank, by reason of his singular vernes, and as it were almost to bee had in admiration, as hereafter you shall vnderstand. And for that none suche as of auncient time, or of late dayes, haue written the nature of plantes, did neuer make mention thereof, I haue therefore learned the whole historie touching the same, which I learned of a gentleman my very friend, the first authour, inuenter, and bringer of this hearb into France : wherfore I thought good to publish it in writing for their sakes, that haue so often hearde speaking of this saide hearbe, and yet neyther knew the hearbe nor the effectes thereof.

This Hearbe is called *Nicotiane*, of the name of him that gaue the firste intelligence thereof vnto this Realme, as many other plantes haue taken their names of certayne Greekes and Romaynes, who hauing beene in straunge Countries, for seruice of their common Weales, haue brought into their countries many plants, which were before vnknowne. Some haue called this

Hearbe the Queenes Hearbe, because it was firste sent vnto her, as heere-after shalbe declared by the Gentleman, that was the first inuenter of it, and since was by her geuen to diuers for to sowe, whereby it might bee planted in this lande. Others haue named it the great Priors hearbe, for that he caused it to multiply in Fraunce, more then any other, for the greate reuerence that he bare to (t)his hearbe, for the Diuine effectes therin contayned. Many haue geuen it the name, *Petum*, which is indeede the proper name of the Hearbe, as they which haue trauelled that Countrie can tell. Notwithstanding, it is better to name it *Nicotiane*, by the name of him that sent it into Fraunce first, to the ende that hee may haue the honour thereof, according to his desert, for that hee hath enriched our Countrie [*i.e.* France], with so singular an Hearbe. Thus much for the name, and nowe hearken further for the whole Historie.

    Then follows NICOT'S own account :

    Maister Iohn *Nicot*, Counseller to the King, being Embassadour for his Maiestie in Portugall, in the yeere of our Lorde. 1559. 60. 61. went one day to see the Prysons of the King of Portugall: and a Gentleman beeyng the keeper of the sade Prisons presented him with this hearb, as a strange Plant brought from *Florida*. The same Maister *Nicot*, hauing caused the said hearb to be set in his Garden, where it grewe and multiplied maruellously, was vppon a time aduertised, by one of his Pages, that a young man, of kinne to that Page made asaye of that hearbe brused both the hearbe and the Iuice together vppon an vlcer, which he had vpon his cheeke neere vnto his nose, comming of a *Noli me tangere*, which began to take roote already at the gristles of the Nose, wherewith hee founde himselfe meruellously eased. Therefore the sayde Maister *Nicot* caused the sicke young man to bee brought before him, and causing the saide hearb to be continued to the sore eight or ten daies, this saide *Noli me tangere*, was vtterly extinguished and healed : and he had sent it, while this cure was a woorking to a certeine Phisition of the King of Portugall one of the greatest fame to examine the further working and effect of the said *Nicotiane*, and sending for the same young man at the end of ten dayes, the sayde Phisition seeing the visage of the said sicke yong man, certified, that the sayde *Noli me tangere* was vtterly extinguished, as in deede he neuer felt it since.

    Within a while after, one of the Cookes of the sayde Embassadour hauing almost cutte off his thombe, with a great chopping knyfe, the Steward of the house of the sayde Gentleman ran to the sayde *Nicotiane*, and dressed him therewith fiue or sixe tymes, and so in the ende thereof he was healed : from that time forward this hearbe began to bee famous throughout *Lishebron*, where the court of the kyng of Portugall was at that present, and the vertue of this sayde hearbe was extolled, and the people began to name it the Ambassadours hearbe. Wherefore there came certaine dayes after a Gentleman of the Countrie, Father to one of the Pages of the Ambassadour, who was troubled with an vlcer in his Legge, hauinge had the same twoo yeeres, and demaunded of the sayde Ambassadour for his hearbe, and vsing the same in such order as is before written, at the end of tenne or twelue daies hee was healed. From that tyme forth the fame of that same hearbe increased in such sort, that many came from al places to haue some of it. Among al others there was a woman that had her face couered wyth a Ringworme rooted, as though she had a Visour on her face, to whome she saide L[ord] Embassadour caused the hearbe to be giuen, and told how she should vse it, and at the ende of eight or tenne daies, this woman was throughly healed, who came and presented her selfe to the Ambassadour, shewing him of her healing.

    After there came a Captaine to present his Sonne sick of the kinges euill to the sayde L[ord] Ambassadour, for to send him into France, vnto whome there was asaye made of the sayde hearbe, which in fewe dayes did begin to shewe great signes of healing, and finally he was altogether healed therby of the kings euill.

    The L[ord] Ambassadour seeing so great effectes proceeding of this hearbe, and hauing heard say that the Lady Montigue that was, dyed at Saint *Germans*, of an vlcer bredd in her brest, that did turne to a *Noli me tangere*,

for the which there could neuer remedy bee founde, and lykewyse that the
Countesse of *Ruff*, had sought for al the famous Phisitions of that Realme,
for to heale her face, vnto whom they could giue no remedy, he thought it
good to communicate the same into France, and did sende it to king
Frauncis the seconde, and to the Queene Mother, and to many other Lords
of the Court, with the maner of ministring the same: and howe to apply it
vnto the said diseases, euen as he had found it by experience, and chiefly to
the Lorde of *Iarnac* gouernour of Rogel, with whom the saide Lorde Am-
bassadour had great amitie for the seruice of the king. The which Lord
of *Iarnac* said one day at the Queenes table, yat he had caused the saide
Nicotiane to be distilled, and the water to bee dronke, mingled with water
Euphrasie, otherwise called eyebright, to one that was shorte breathed, who
was therewith healed. . . .

[*Here follow descriptions of the herb, and directions for its cultivation.*]

Moreouer the inhabitantes of *Florida* do nourish themselues certaine
ymes, with the smoke of this Hearbe, which they receaue at the mouth
through certaine coffins, suche as the Grocers do vse to put in their Spices.
There be other oyntmentes prepared of the sayde hearbe, with other simples,
but for a truth this only simple hearbe, taken and applyed as aforesayde, is of
greater efficacie, notwithstanding one may make thereof an oyntment, which
is singular, to cleanse, incarnate, and knit together al maner of woundes:
the making of the sayde Oyntmente is thus. Take a pounde of the freshe
leaues of the sayde Hearbe, stampe them, and mingle them with newe Waxe,
Rosine, common oyle, of eche three ounces, let them boyle altogether, vntil
the luyce *Nicotiane* be consumed, then adde therto three ounces of *Venise*
Turpentine, straine the same through a Linen cloth, and keepe it in Pottes
to your vse.

Liébaut thus concludes :—

Loe, here you haue the true Historie of *Nicotiane*, of the whiche the sayde
Lorde *Nicot*. one of the Kynges Counsellers first founder out of this hearbe,
hath made mee priuie aswell by woorde as by wryting, to make thee friendly
Reader partaker therof, to whom I require thee to yeeld as harty thankes
as I acknowledge my self bounde vnto him, for this benefite receiued.—*Joyfull News*, fol. 42-45.

In so far therefore, as these two editions of *Joyfull newes* cir-
culated, this much was known in England respecting Tobacco,
so early as 1577-80.

II. The principal notices of the first introduction of the Herb
into this country are these :—

1. EDMUND HOWES, in his continuation of J. Stow's *Annales*,
[p. 1038. Ed. 1631] states—

Tobacco was first brought, and made known in England by Sir Iohn
Hawkins, about the yeare 1565 but not vsed by Englishmen in many yeeres
after, though at this day commonly vsed by most men, and many women.

The dates of Mr, afterwards Sir John Hawkins' voyages to the
West Indies, are

The first	Oct. 1562—	Sept. 1563.
The second	18 Oct. 1564—20 Sept. 1565.	
The third	} 2 Oct. 1567—25 Jan. 1568.	
' the troublesome voyadge '		

The account of the Second voyage, by John Sparke the younger,
states that Hawkins, ranging along the coast of Florida for fresh
water in July 1565, came upon the French settlement there under
Laudoniere: and in describing that country Sparke mentions that
the natives—

The *Floridians* when they trauell haue a kinde of herbe dryed, which with a cane, and an earthen cup in the end, with fire and the dried herbs put together, do sucke thorow the cane the smoke thereof, which smoke satisfieth their hunger, and therewith they liue foure or fiue dayes without meat or drinke, and this all the Frenchmen vsed for this purpose: yet do they holde opinion withall, that it causeth water and fleame to void from their stomacks.—*Hakluyt, p.* 541. *Ed.* 1589.

2. Howes, on the fame page as the preceding, ftates—
Apricocks, Mellycatons, Musk-Millions and *Tobacco,* came into England about the 20 yeare of Queene Elizabeth [1577].
And adds in the margin—
Sir Walter Raleigh was the first that brought Tobacco into vse, when all men wondred what it meant.

The date here given, fo far as Tobacco fmoking generally is concerned, muft be wrong by about ten years.

III. Smoking appears to have been firft taught in England, under the following circumftances :—

1. Sir Walter Raleigh's firft Expedition took poffeffion of Virginia on 13 July 1584, and after a fix weeks' ftay in the country, returned home. The next year, a fecond expedition conveyed out a colony under Mafter Ralph Lane, which remained in the country from 17 Aug. 1585 to 18 June 1586: when Sir Francis Drake and his fleet returning from his victorious raid in the Weft Indies brought home the colony to the number of 103 perfons. Among thefe was the celebrated mathematician Thomas Hariot, who in his exceffively rare ' *Briefe and true report of the new found land of Virginia : &c.* . . . . Imprinted at London 1588,' thus defcribes Tobacco, and the adoption of the fmoking of it by thefe Virginian colonifts.

There is an herbe which is sowed a part by it selfe and is called by the inhabitants *vppówoc*: In the West Indies it hath diuers names, according to the seuerall places and countries where it groweth and is vsed: The Spaniardes generally call it *Tobacco.* The leaues thereof being dried and brought into powder : they vse to take the fume or smoke thereof by sucking it through pipes made of claie into their stomacke and heade ; from whence it purgeth superfluous fleame and other grosse humors, openeth all the pores and passages of the body : by which meanes the vse thereof, not only preserueth the body from obstructions; but also if any be, so that they haue not beene of too long continuance, in short time breaketh them : wherby their bodies are notably preserued in health, and know not many greeuous diseases wherewithall wee in England are oftentimes afflicted.

This *Vppówoc* is of so precious estimation amongest them, that they thinke their gods are maruelously delighted therwith : Whereupon sometime they make hallowed fires and cast some of the pouder therein for a sacrifice: being in a storme vppon the waters, to pacifie their gods, they cast some vp into the aire and into the water : so a weare for fish being newly set vp, they cast some therein and into the aire: also after an escape of danger, they cast some into the aire likewise: but all done with strange gestures, stamping, sometime dauncing, clapping of hands, holding vp of hands, and staring vp into the heauens, vttering therewithal and chattering strange words and noises.

We our selues during the time we were there vsed to suck it after their maner, as also since our returne, and haue found manie rare and wonderful experiments of the vertues thereof; of which the relation would require a volume by it felfe: the vse of it by so manie of late, men and women of great calling as else, and some learned Phisitions also, is sufficient witnes.

It would therefore appear that Raleigh himfelf had nothing to do either with the introduction of the weed itfelf, or of the habit of fmoking of it. Hawkins may have brought home a few fpecimens of the plant in 1565; but for the importation of it in any quantity and for the teaching of how to fmoke it, we are indebted to Mafter Ralph Lane and to his fellow-colonifts, who acquired both from the Indians, during the twelve months they were cut off from all intercourfe with their mother-country.

2. William Camden, who was fecond, afterwards Head Mafter of Weftminfter School between 1575-1593, and confequently a contemporary witnefs, in his *Annales*, publifhed in Latin in 1615, at *p.* 388, gives this account; of which this is the earlieft tranfla-tion into Englifh.

These were the first (that I know of) that brought at their returre into *England*, that *Indian* Plant called Tobacco, or *Nicotiana*, which they vsed, being instructed by the *Indians*, against crudities of the Stomack. And certes since that time it is grown so frequent in vse, and of such price, that many, nay, the most part, with an insatiable desire doe take of it, drawing into their mouth the smoke thereof, which is a strong sent, through a Pipe made of earth, and venting of it againe through their nose; some for war.ton-nesse, or rather fashion sake, and other for healths sake, insomuch that To-bacco shops are set vp in greater number than either Alehouses or Tauernes. And as one said, but falsely, the bodies of such Englishmen, as are so much delighted with this plant, did sceme to degenerate into the nature of the Sauages, because they were caried away with the selfe-same thing, beleeuing to obtaine and con erue their health by the selfe-same meanes, as the barbari-ans did.—*Bk. III. p.* 107. *Ed.* 1625.

In the face of thefe facts, attefted by early contemporary tefti-mony: all accounts which reprefent Sir W. Raleigh as introduc-ing Tobacco into England muft be confidered falfe in that refpect.

Incidentally this agrees with the account—though in itfelf no evidence—given in an undated 4 pp. tract, *The Venimous Qua-lities of Tobacco*, apparently printed before 1650.

TABACCO is an ignite Plant, called by the native Americans *Picielt*; by those of *Hispaniola, Pete be Cenuc*: as by those of *New France, Peti, Petum*, and *Petunnm*. It was called by the French *Nicotiana*, from *John Nicotius* Embassador to the king of *France*, who *An.* 1559, first sent this Plant into *France*. But now it is generally by us Europeans termed *Tabaco*, (which we improperly pronounce *Tobacco* a name first given it by the Spani-ards from their Iland *Tabaco*, which abounded with this Plant; whereof had *Plato* had as much experience as we, he would, without al peradventure, have philosophised thereon. They say we are beholding to Sir *Francis Drake*'s Mariners for the knowledge and use of the Plant, who brought its Seed from *Virginie* into *England* about the year 1585.

IV. But while Sir Walter introduced neither the Herb nor the manner of fmoking it, there is a general confent that he princi-pally brought the habit of Tobacco-fmoking, or, as it was at firft called, Tobacco-*drinking*, into fafhion. His name, and his al-moft exclufively, became identified with the new National Habit.

Yet even of this, we have but little demonftrative proof.

It may, however, be well to give fome of the principal traditions and legends on this point.

1. JOHN AUBREY, F. R. S., in his Minutes of *Lives of Eminent Men*, of which his Introductory letter to Anthony à Wood is dated 15 June 1680, gives the following in his life of Raleigh.

He was the first that brought tobacco into England, and into fashion. In our part of North Wilts—*e. g.* Malmesbury hundred—it came first into fashion by Sir Walter Long. They had first silver pipes. The ordinary sort made use of a walnut shell and a strawe. I have heard my grandfather Lyte say, that one pipe was handed from man to man round the table. Sir W. Raleigh standing in a stand at Sir Robert Poyntz parke, at Acton, tooke a pipe of tobacco, which made the ladies quitt it till he had donne. Within these 35 years, 'twas scandalous for a divine to take tobacco. It was sold then for its wayte in siluer. I haue heard some of our old yeomen neighbours say, that when they went to Malmesbury or Chippenham Market, they culled out their biggest shillings to lay in the scales against the tobacco; now, the customes of it are the greatest his majestie hath.—*Letters written by Eminent Persons.* Ed. by John Aubrey. *ii.* 512. *Ed.* 1813.

2. J. P. MALCOLM, in his *Londinium Redivivum, iv. p.* 490, *Ed.* 1801, states.
'There was a tradition, in the parish of St. Matthew, Friday Street, that Sir Walter Raleigh and Sir Hugh Myddleton often smoaked tobacco together at the door of Sir Hugh's house' in that parish.

3. THOMAS PENNANT, in his *Journey to Snowdon, p.* 28, *Ed.* 1781, which forms the second volume of his *Tour in Wales*, the first of which was published in 1778; gives the following account of William Middleton: the third son of Richard Middleton, Governor of Denbigh Castle, and brother to Sir Hugh Middleton, the fixth son in that family.

The particular information, from 'It is fayd' to †, is given on the authority of the *Sebright MSS.*, *i.e.* MSS. formerly belonging to Mr. Edward Lloyd, but lent to him by Sir John Sebright, Bart., in whose poffeffion they were, at the date of Pennant's preface, 1 March 1781. The last part of the paragraph is merely Pennant's speculation: but there may be fome truth in the MS. legend.

The third, *William*, was a sea captain, and an eminent poet. His early education was at *Oxford:* but his military turn led him abroad, where he signalized himself as soldier and sailor. He translated the psalms into *Welsh* metre, and finished them on *Jan.* 4th, 1595, *apud* Scutum *insulam occidentalium Iudorum*; which, as well as his *Barddoniaeth*, or art of *Welsh* poetry, were published in *London;* the first in 1603, the other in 1593. It is sayed, that he, with captain *Thomas Price*, of *Plâsyollin*, and one captain *Koet*, were the first who smoked, or (as they called it) drank tobacco publickly in *London;* and that the *Londoners* flocked from all parts to see them.† Pipes were not then invented, so they used the twisted leaves, or *segars*. The invention is usually ascribed to Sir *Walter Raleigh*. It may be so; but he was too good a courtier to smoke in public, especially in the reign of *James*, who even condescended to write a book against the practice, under the title of *The Counter-blast to Tobacco.*

4. A Phyfician [Dr. J. A. PARIS] in *A Guide to Mounts Bay and Lands End, p.* 39, *Ed.* 1824, states.

A tradition exists here, that *Tobacco* was first smoked by *Sir Walter Raleigh* in Penzance. on his land ng from America.

Which legend is quite contrary to the facts.

5. WILLIAM OLDYS, in his Life of Sir Walter Raleigh prefixed to *The History of the World*, Ed. 1736, xxvii., gives the following from a 4to MS. entitled *Apophthegms of the English Nation*, then in the collection of Rodney Fane, Esq.

He [Sir W. Raleigh] assured her majesty [Queen Elizabeth] he had so well experienced the nature of it, that he could tell her of what weight even the sm ke would be in any quantity prop- s'd to be con-um'd. Her majesty fixing her thoughts upon the most practicable part of the experiment, that ' f bounding the *smoke* in a *ballance*, suspected the: he put the traveller upon her, and would needs lay him a wager he cou'd not solve the doubt: so he procured a quantity agreed upon to be thoroughly smok'd. then went to weighing; but it was of the ashes; and in the conclusion, what was wanting in the pri e we'ght of the tobacco, her majesty did n t deny to have been evaporated in smoke; and further said, that *many labourers in the fire she had heard of who turned their gold into smoke, but* Ralegh *was the first who had turned smoke into gold.*

JAMES HOWELL, *Familiar Letters*, iii. 12, *Ed.* 1650, in a Letter on Tobacco, incidentally confirms this story.

But if one would try a pretty conclusion how much smoak ther is in a pound of Tobacco, the ashes will tell him; for let a pound be exactly weighed, and the ashe, kept charily and weighed afterwards, what wants of a pound weight in the ashes cannot be denied to have bin smoak, which evaporated into air: I haue bin t ld that Sir Walter Rawleigh won a wager of Queen *Elizabeth* upon this nicity.

6. We have now come to a legend, perhaps the most untrustworthy of all.

(1.) In *Tarlton's Jests*, 1611, 4to, there occurs the following story.

How Tarlton tooke tobacco at the first comming up of it.

Tarlton, as other gentlemen used, at the first comming up of tobacco, did take it more for fashion's sake than otherwise; and being in a roome, set between two men overcome with wine, and they never seeing the like, wondred at t. and seeing the vapour come out of Tarlton's nose, cryed out: fire, fire! and threw a cup of wine in Tarlton's face. Make no more stirre, quoth Tarlton. the fire is quenched; if the sheriffes come, it will turne to a fine. as the custome is. And drinking that againe: fie, sayes the other, what a stinke it makes; I am almost poysoned. If it offend, saies Tarlton, let's every one take a little of the smell, and so the savour will quickly goe: but tobacco whiffes made them leave him to pay all.—*Shakespeare's Jest-Books*, Ed. by W. C. Hazlitt. *ii.* 221. *Ed.* 1864.

(2.) In 1619, BARNABY RICH inserted in the *second* edition of *The Irish Hubbub, or the English Hue and Crie*, a similar story.

I remember a pretty iest of Tobacco. That was this. A certaine Welchman comming newly to London, and beholding one to take tobacco. neuer seeing the like before, and not knowing the manner of it, but perceiuing him vent smoake so fast, and supposing his inward parts to be on fire: cried out, O Ihesu, Ihesu man. for the passion of Cod hold, for by Cods splud ty snowts on fire, and hauing a bowle of beere in his hand, threw it at the others face to quench his smoking nose.—*p.* 45.

(3.) To somewhat similar purport is the legend of Sir W. Raleigh and the Tankard of Ale. Of this story, though evidently current in the seventeenth century, Oldys could quote no earlier authority than *The British Apollo*, 3d Ed. *p.* 376, London 1726: and we can only adduce the authority of the firſt edition of the ſame work.

The Britiſh Apollo was a bi-weekly periodical ' Perform'd by a Society of Gentlemen,' partly devoted to the explanation of difficulties in Divinity, Mathematics, Love, and ſuch like, and partly to Poetry and Political News. In itſelf of no authority whatever, it merely diſpenſed its modicums of current knowledge from the learned to the general public.

In Vol. I, No. 43, publiſhed on July 7, 1708, occur the following queſtion and anſwer.

Q. Gentlemen, Pray how long is it since, the smoaking Tobacco, and the taking Snuff hath been in Use here in England; *the time when they were first brought over, and how, or by whom.* Your Humble Servant, H. S.

A. Snuff, tho' the Use of it has been long known to such, as were by merchandizing or other means, familiar with the Spanish Customes, has been till lately a perfect Stranger to the Practice of the British Nation, and like our other Fashions came to us from *France*, but the Use of Tobacco-smoaking, was introduc'd by Sir *Walter Rawleigh*, in the Reign of Queen *Elizabeth*; and since a comical story depends upon the Relation, it may not be unacceptable to the Querist and the Publick.

Sir *Walter* having imitated the *Indians* by delighting in their Favorite Weed, was unwilling to disuse it, and therefore at his return to *England*, supplied himself with some Hogsheads, which he plac'd in his own Study, and generally indulg'd himself in Smoaking secretly, two Pipes a Day: at which times he order'd a Simple Fellow, who waited at his Study Door, to bring him up a Tankard of old Ale and Nutmeg, always laying aside the Pipe, when he heard his Servant coming : But while he was one day, earnestly imploy'd in Reading something, which amus'd him, The Fellow enter'd, and surprizing his Master, as the Smoak ascended thickly from his Mouth and the Bole of the Pipe, he threw the Ale directly in his Face ; and running down Stairs alarm'd the Family with repeated Exclamations, that his Master was on fire in the in-side, and before they could get up Stairs would be burnt to Ashes.

How much this legend wanders from the facts of the caſe, will be apparent from the above. There may, however, be earlier accounts of this ſtory in a more credible form : but we have not met with them. The ſtory may poſſibly have been connected with other names beſides Tarleton, the Welſhman, and Raleigh.

Oldys, in quoting the legend, remarks.

This I say, if true, has nothing in it of more surprising or unparallel'd simplicity, than there was in that poor *Norwegian*, who upon the first sight of *Roses* could not be induced to *touch*, tho' he saw them *grow*, being so amazed to behold *trees budding with fire*; or, to come closer by way of retaliation, than there was in those *Virginians* themselves, who, the first time they seized upon a quantity of *Gun-powder* which belong'd to the *English* colony, *sow'd it for grain*, or the seed of some strange vegetable in the earth, with full expectation of reaping a plentiful crop of combustion by the next harvest to scatter their enemies. *Life of Sir W. Raleigh, xx.xi. Ed.* 1736.

6. We may conclude this ſtring of ſtories, with a truſtworthy account of Sir W. Raleigh's Tobacco Box. OLDYS in his *Life*, xxxi. Note e, Ed. 1736, tells us, that

Being at *Leeds* in *Yorkshire*, soon after Mr. *Ralph Thoresby* the antiquary died, *Anno* 1725. I saw his *Musæum*; and in it, among other rarities, what himself has publickly call'd (in the *catalogue* thereof, annexed to his *antiquities* of that town) Sir *Walter Ralegh's* tobacco box. From the best of my memory, I can resemble its outward appearance to nothing more nearly than one of our modern *Muff-cases;* about the same height and width, cover'd with red leather, and open'd at top but with a hinge. I think like one of those. In the inside, there was a cavity for a receiver of glass or metal, which might hold half a pound or a pound of tobacco; and from the edge of the receiver at top, to the edge of the box, a circular stay or collar, with holes in it, to plant the tobacco about, with six or eight pipes to smoke it in. This travelling box, with the MSS. Medals and other rarities in its company, descending to a young clergyman, the son of the deceased, was soon after reported to have been translated to *London.*

V. The general credence and affociation of Smoking with Sir W. Raleigh being remembered; may it not be taken as proof of a malignancy towards him—even thus early—on the part of the Writer of the *Counterblaste ;* in that he depreciates ' the firft Author' as neither King, great Conqueror, nor learned Doctor of Phyficke,' and affirms the cuftome to be ' brought in by a father fo generally hated;' in that he wilfully or ignorantly falfifies the hiftory of the Introduction of Tobacco; concocting a degrading ftory for his purpofe.

VI. We have now but to notice the early beginnings of the Tobacco Controverfy, which—fometimes flumbering, fometimes raging—has lafted to our own time, and will yet go on. It created a larger early Tobacco literature in England than is generally thought, or than we have been able to trace. It raged over Europe as well as in England.

And here we may exprefs fome aftonifhment that no one among the countlefs myriads of Smokers, has ever written a Hiftory of the Tobacco Literature and of the progrefs of Smoking through civilized and uncivilized communities, even unto this laft age, wherein the Whahabees of Arabia punifh it, under the name of *Drinking the fhameful* with death. Of fketches there are feveral. Mr. F. Tiedeman has given an excellent one of the general Introduction of the plant into Europe, in his *Gefchichte des Tabaks, etc.,* Frankfort, 1852. Mr. F. W. Fairholt in his *Hiftory of Tobacco,* London 1842, has given a good inftalment towards a Hiftory of the fubject: while *A Paper: of Tobacco,* by Jofeph Fume [W. A. Chatto] London, 1832, is a flighter ftudy ftill. Another work, *A Pinch of Snuff,* London, 1837, I have been unable to meet with. Dr. H. W. Cleland in his privately printed work *On the Hiftory and Properties, Chemical and Medical, of Tobacco,* Glasgow, July 1840—which work also we have not had the advantage of confulting—gives a lift of 150 works on this fubject. All thefe modern works are but helps to the future Hiftorian of Tobacco.

VII. To thefe ; we can add here but another fketch of the earlier Controverfy; and that a very limited one. It will be convenient to give the notices under each year: dwelling more particularly on thofe which incidentally illuftrate the growth of the Habit, as well as the progrefs of the Controverfy. .

1587. *De Herba Panacea*, written by GILES EVARARD, latinized ÆGIDIUS EVERARDUS, may be juft mentioned : becaufe it formed the text of a larger Englifh work, *Panacea* : publifhed in London in 1659.

1595. WILLIAM BARLEY had a licence to print a Treatife defcribing the nature of Tobacco. *Herbert's Ames, ii. 277.*

1596. BEN JONSON, in *Every Man in his Humour*, Act III. Sc. 2, acted on 25th November 1596, thus very skilfully reprefents both sides of the controversy, in the speeches of *Bobadilla* and *Cob.*

Bobadilla. Body of me : here's the remainder of seuen pound, since yesterday was seuennight. It's your right *Trinidado* : did you neuer take any, signior ?

Stephano. No truly sir ? but i'le learne to take it now, since you commend it so.

Bobadilla. Signior beleeue me, (vpon my relation' for what I tel you, the world shall not improue. I haue been in the Indies (where this herbe growes) where neither my selfe, nor a dozen Gentlemen more of my knowledge' haue receiued the taste of any other nutriment, in the world, for the space of one and twentie weekes, but Tabacco onely. Therefore it cannot be but 'tis most diuine. Further, take it in the nature, in the true kinde so, it makes an Antidote, that had you taken the most deadly poysonous simple in all Florence, it should expell it, and clarifie you, with as much ease, as I speak. And for your greene wound, your *Balsamum*, and your —— are all meere gulleries, and trash to it, especially your *Trinidado* ; your *Newcotian* is good too : I could say what I know of the vertue of it, for the exposing of rewmes, raw humors, crudities, obstructions, with a thousand of this kind ; but I professe my selfe no quacke-saluer : only thus much : by *Hercules* I doe holde it, and will affirme it (before any Prince in Europe) to be the most foueraigne, and pretious herbe, that euer the earth tendred to the vse of man.

Immediately afterwards ; he makes *Cob* reprefent the other side.

Cob. By gods deynes : I marle what pleasure or felicitie they haue in taking this rogish Tabacco : it's good for nothing but to choake a man, and fill him full of smoake, and imbers : there were foure died out of one house last weeke with taking of it, and two more the bell went for yester-night, one of them (they say) will ne're scape it, he voyded a bushell of soote yester-day, vpward and downeward   By the stockes ; and there were no wiser men then I, I'ld haue it present death, man or woman, that should but deale with a Tabacco pipe ; why, it will stifle them all in the'nd as many as vse it ; it's little better than rats bane. *Ed.* 1601.

(3.) Tobacco is faid not to be alluded to by Shakefpeare or in the *Arabian Nights.*

(4.) It is often noticed by other Englifh dramatifts : as Dekker and others later on.   See alfo Malone, *Hift. Acc. of the Englifh Stage, p. 584.*

1597. THOMAS GERARD, 'Master in Chiurvrgerie,' figures and defcribes the Tobacco plant in *The Herbal or General Hiftoire of Plantes*, Bk. ii. pp. 285-9.

1597. Bp. JOSEPH HALL publifhes his Satires, in which he alludes to Tobacco Smoking, Bk. iv. Sat. 4 ; Bk. v. Sat. 2.

1598. PAUL HENTZNER, in his Latin *Itinerarium* under Auguft 1598, has a paffage, of which the following is a tranflation by Mr. W. B. Rye :—

At these spectacles, and everywhere else, the English are constantly smoking the Nicotian weed, which in America is called *Tobaca*—others call it *Pætum*—[*i.e. Petun*, the Brazilian name for Tobacco, from which the allied beautiful plant 'Petunia' derives its appellati-n,] and generally in this manner: they have pipes on purpose made of clay, into the farther end of which they put the herb, so dry that it may be rubbed into powder, and lighting it, they draw the smoke into their mouths, which they puff out again through their nostrils like funnels, along with it plenty of phlegm and defluxion from the head.—*England as seen by Foreigners, p.* 216, *ed.* 1865.

1599. HENRY BUTTES, M.A. and Fellow of C.C.C., in C[ambridge], wrote a strange work, *Diets Dry Dinner,* of which title he gives this explanation—

Dyets dry Dinner. That is, varietie of Fare: prouided, prepared and ordered, at *Dyets* own prescription: whose seruant and Attendant at this feast I professe my selfe. Thus far perhaps not disliked of any. A *Dry Dinner,* not only *Caninum Prandium,* without Wine, but *Accipitrinum,* without all drinke except *Tabacco,* (which also is but Dry Drinke): herein not like to be liked of many. What ere it be as he saith in the Comedie) *Habeas et Naeta,* take it as you finde it, and welcome. More then which I cannot perform.

The following preface *To my Country-men Readers,* is so allusive that its entire insertion may be pardoned, though it wander a little from our subject:—

Welcome courteous Countreymen. I meane especially *Norfolkmen.* For they are true Catholiques in matter of Dyet: no Recusants of any thing that is mans meate. I bid all in general, excepting only such as are affrayed of roasted Pigge, a breast or legge of Mutton, a Ducke &c. To conclude, I forbid no man, but him onely that hath maried a wife and cannot come. No man shall loose his labour. Here are *Lettuses* for euery mans lips. For the *Northeren-man, White-meates, Beefe, Mutton, Venison:* for the *Southerne-man, Fruites, Hearbes, Fowle, Fish, Spice,* and *Sauce.* As for the *Middle-sex* or *Londoner,* I smell his Diet. *Vescitur aura aetheria.* Here is a Pipe of right *Trinidado* for him. The *Yorkers* they will be content with bald *Tabacodocko.* What should I say? here is good *Veale* for the *Essex-man:* passing *Leekes* and excellent *Cheese* for the *Welsh-man. Denique quid non?* Mary, here are neither *Eg-pies* for the *Lancashire-man,* nor *Wag-tayles* for the *Kentish-man.* But that is all one, here is other good cheere enough. And what is wanting in meate, shall bee supplyed in kinde welcome and officious attendance.

Least any thing should be amisse, or missing to thee, I haue my selfe (for fault of a better taken vpon me all such Offices as any way concerne this Dinner.

1 CHOISE. First, I am *Cator*: and haue prouided the very choise of such daynties as Natures Market affoordeth.

2 VSE. Secondly, I am *Taster*: commending each dish to thy Palate, according to his right vse and vertue.

3 HURT. And (since nothing is so perfectly good, as it partaketh of no euill pr-perty) I haue put into a by-dish like *Eg-shelles* in a Saucer what worthily may breed offence. Herein imitating a merry *Greeke,* who espying an haire in a dish of Butter, called for another dish and dished it by it self.

4 PREPARATION or CORRECTION. Thirdly, I play the *Cooke*: so preparing, seasoning, and saucing the harmefull disposition of euery meat, as it shall be either in whole abolished, or in part qualified.

[5] DEGREE, SEASON, AGE, CONSTITUTION. Lastly, I assume the *Caruers* office: and hauing noted the nature and operation of each particular dispense to euery of my Guests according to the Season, his Age, and Constitution.

Thus very rudely, I obtrude vnto thee not a banquet, but a byt rather of each dish *Scholler-likely,* that is, badly carued. For *Schollers are bad Caruers.* Do thou, by thy kindly feeding on *Dyets dry Dinner,* but cause thy selfe to thirst for *Dyets Drinking:* and I shall with like alacrity, act thy *Cup-bearer.* Wherefore vntill thou beest Dry drunke, Fare-well. *Thy Countryman.* H. Buttes.

Applying his method, Buttes thus difcourfes of Tabacco :

CHOISE. Translated out of India in the seed or roote ; Natiue or satiue in our own fruitfullest soiles : Dried in the shade, and compiled very close : of a tawny colour, somwhat inclining to red : most perspicuous and cleare : which the Nose soonest taketh in snuffe.

VSE. It cureth any griefe, dolour, opilation, impostume, or obstruction, proceeding of cold or winde : especially in the head or breast : the leaues are good against the Migram, cold stomackes, sick kidnies, tooth-ache, fits of the moother, naughty breath, scaldings or burnings : 4. ounces of the iuyce drunk, purgeth vp and downe : cleanseth the eyes, being outwardly applied. The water distilled and taken afore the fits, cureth an Ague.

The fume taken in a Pipe is good against Rumes, Catarrhs, hoarsenesse, ache in the head, stomacke, lungs, breast : also in want of meat, drinke, sleepe, or rest.

HURT. Mortifieth and benummeth ; causeth drowsinesse : troubleth and dulleth the sences : makes (as it were) drunke : dangerous in meale time.

CORRECTION. The leaues be-ashed or warmed in imbers and ashes : taken once a day at most, in ye morning, fasting.

DEGREE. Hot and dry in the second : of a stiffening and soddering nature. Also disensing and dissoluing filthy humours, consisting of contrary qualities.

SEASON. AGE. CONSTITUTION. In Winter and the Spring, for hot, strong, youthful, and fat bodies only, as some thinke.

Buttes alfo compofes *A Satyricall Epigram, vpon the wanton, and exceffiue vfe of Tabacco.*

> IT chaunc'd me gazing at the Theater,
> To spie a Lock-Tabacco-Chevalier,
> Clowding the loathing ayr with foggie fume
> Of Dock-Tabacco, friendly foe to rume.
> I wisht the Roman lawes seuerity :   *Alex. seu. Edict.*
> *Who smoke selleth, with smoke be don to dy.*
> Being well nigh smouldred with his smokie stir,
> I gan this wize bespeak my gallant Sir :
> Certes, me thinketh (Sir) it ill beseems,
> Thus here to vapour out these reeking steams :
> Like or to *Maroes* steeds, whose nosthrils flam'd ;
> Or *Plinies* Nosemen (mouthles men) surnam'd,
> Whose breathing nose supply'd Mouths absency.
> He me regreets with this prophane reply :
> Nay ; I resemble (Sir) *Jehouah* dread,
> From out whose nosthrils a smoake issued :
> Or the mid-ayrs congealed region,
> Whose stomach with crude humors frozenon
> Sucks vp Tabacco-like the vpmost ayr,
> Enkindled by Fires neighbour candle fayr :
> And hence it spits out watry reums amaine,
> As phleamy snow, and haile, and sheerer raine :
> Anon it smoakes beneath, it flames anon.
> Sooth then, quoth I, it's safest we be gon,
> Lest there arise some *Ignis Fatuus*
> From out this smoaking flame, and choken vs.
>   On English foole ; wanton Italianly :
>   Go Frenchly : Duchly drink : breath Indianly.

He then gives this *Storie for Table-talke.*

This Hearbe is of great Antiquitie and high respect among the Indians, and especially those of *America* or new *Spain.* Of whom the Spaniards tooke it, after they had subdued those Countries, first vpon a liking of the hearbe verie faire and glorious to the eye ; afterward vpon triall of his vertues worthie admiration.

The Name in *India* is *Pilciet,* surnamed *Tabacco* by the Spaniard, of the ile *Tabaco*. By their meanes it spred farre and neare : but yet wee are not beholden to their tradition. Our English *Vlisses*, renomed Syr *Walter Rawleigh*, a man admirably excellent in Nauigation, of Natures priuy counsell, and infinitely reade in the wide booke of the worlde, hath both farre fetcht it, and deare bought it : the estimate of the treasure I leaue to other : yet this a'l know, since it came in request, there hath bene *Magnus fumi questus*, and *Fumi-vendulus* is the best Epithite for an Apothecary.

Thus much late Histories tell vs : among the Indians it is so highly honoured, that when the Priests are consulting in matter of importance, they presently cast Tabacco into the fire, and receiue at their nose and mouth, the smoak through a Cane, till they fall downe dead-drunke. Afterward reuiuing againe, they giue answeres according to the phantasmes and visions, which appeared to them in their sleepe.

1602. (1) "*Work for Chimney-fweepers : or A warning for To-bacconifts*. Defcribing the pernicious vfe of *Tobacco*, no leffe pleafant than profitable for all forts to reade : *Fumus patriæ, Igne alieno Luculentior*. As much to fay, Better be chokt with Englifh hemp, then poifoned with Indian Tabacco." Written by PHILARETES, who alleges eight reafons againft Tobacco ; whereof one is—

7 Seauenthly, for that the first author and finder hereof was the Diuell, and the first practisers of the same were the Diuells Priests, and therefore not to be vsed of vs Christians.

(2.) This provoked "*A Defence of Tabacco :* with a friendly answer to the late printed Booke called *Worke for Chimney-Sweepers. Si indicas, cognofe : fi Rex es, iube.*"

(3.) Sir WILLIAM VAUGHAN, in his *Naturall and Artificiall Directions for health, &c.* Sect. ii. ch. 8. *Of Hearbes. p.* 22.

Cane *Tabacco* well dryed, and taken in a siluer pipe, fasting in the morning, cureth the megrim, the tooth ache, obstructions proceeding of cold, and helpeth the fits of the mother. After meales it doth much hurt, for it infecteth the braine and the liues.

In his fourth edition of this work, publifhed in 1613, he altered his mind and wrote againft Smoking.

(4.) Another anonymous work dedicated 'To my loving Friend Mafter Michael Drayton,' appeared, entitled *The Metamorphofis of Tabacco.* It opens with the following lines :—

> I sing the loues of the superiour powers,
> With the faire mother of all fragrant flowers :
> From which first loue a glorious Simple springs,
> Belou'd of heau'nly Gods, and earthly Kings.
> Let others in their wanton verses chaunt
> A beautious face that doth their senses daunt,
> And on their Muses wings lift to the skie
> The radiant beames of an inchaunting eye.
> Me let the sound of great *Tabaccoes* praise
> A pitch aboue those loue-sicke Poets raise :
> Let me adore with my thrice-happie pen
> The sweete and sole delight of mortall men,
> The *Cornu-copia* of all earthly pleasure,
> Where bank-rupt Nature hath consum'd her treasure,
> A worthie plant springing from *Floraes* hand,
> The blessed ofspring of an vncouth land.

1604. In the course of this year ; there was anonymoufly publifhed

A
COVNTER-
BLASTE TO
Tobacco.

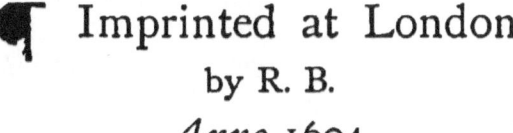

Imprinted at London
by R. B.
Anno 1604.

¶ To The Reader.

S euery humane body (*deare Countrey men*) *how wholesome soeuer, is notwithstanding subiect, or at least naturally inclined to some sorts of diseases, or infirmities: so is there no Common-wealth, or Body-politicke, how* well gouerned, or peaceable soeuer it bee. that lackes the owne popular errors, and naturally enclined corruptions: and therefore is it no wonder, although this our Countrey and Common-wealth, though peaceable, though wealthy, though long flourishing in both, be amongst the rest, subiect to the owne naturall infirmities. VVe are of all Nations the people most louing and most reuerently obedient to our Prince, yet are wee (as time hath often borne witnesse) too easie to be seduced to make Rebellion, vpon very slight grounds. Our fortunate and oft prooued valour in warres abroad, our heartie and reuerent obedience to our Princes at home, hath bred vs a long, and a thrice happy peace: Our Peace hath bred wealth: And Peace and wealth hath brought foorth a generall sluggishnesse, which makes vs wallow in all sorts of idle delights, and soft delicacies, the first seedes of the subuersion of all great Monarchies. Our Cleargie are become negligent and lazie, our Nobilitie and Gentrie prodigall, and solde to

their priuate delights, Our Lawyers couetous, our Com-
mon-people prodigall and curious; and generally all sorts
of people more carefull for their priuat ends, then for
their mother the Common-wealth.

For remedie whereof, it is the Kings *part (as the pro-*
per Phisician of his Politicke-body) to purge it of all those
diseases, by Medicines meete for the same : as by a certaine
milde, and yet iust forme of gouernment, to maintaine the
Publicke quietnesse, and preuent all occasions of Commo-
tion : by the example of his owne Person and Court, to
make vs all ashamed of our sluggish delicacie, and to
stirre vs vp to the practise againe of all honest exer-
cises, and Martiall shadowes of VVarre; As like-
wise by his, and his Courts moderatenesse in Apparell,
to make vs ashamed of our prodigalitie : By his quicke
admonitions and carefull ouerseeing of the Cleargie, to
waken them vp againe, to be more diligent in their Offices :
By the sharpe triall, and seuere punishment of the partiall,
couetous and bribing Lawyers, to reforme their corruptions:
And generally by the example of his owne Person, and
by the due execution of good Lawes, to reforme and abolish,
piece and piece, these old and euill grounded abuses. For
this will not bee Opus vnius diei, *but as euery one of these*
diseas's, must from the King *receiue the owne cure proper*
for it, so are there some sorts of abuses in Common-
wealths, that though they be of so base and contemptible
a condition, as they are too low for the Law to looke on,
and too meane for a King *to interpone his authoritie, or*
bend his eye vpon : yet are they corruptions, aswell as the
greatest of them. So is an Ant an Animal, *aswell as an*
Elephant : so is a VVrenne Auis, *aswell as a Swanne;*
and so is a small dint of the Toothake, a disease aswe
as the fearefull Plague is. But for these base sorts of
corruption in Common-wealthes, not onely the King, *or*

G

any inferior Magiſtrate, but Quilibet è populo *may ſerue to be a Phiſician, by diſcouering and impugning the error, and by perſwading reformation thereof.*

And ſurely in my opinion, there cannot be a more baſe, and yet hurtfull, corruption in a Countrey, then is the vile vſe (or other abuſe) of taking Tobacco *in this Kingdome, which hath mooued me, ſhortly to diſcouer the abuſes thereof in this following little Pamphlet.*

If any thinke it a light Argument, ſo is it but a toy that is beſtowed vpon it. And ſince the Subiect is but of Smoke, I thinke the fume of an idle braine, may ſerue for a ſufficient battery against ſo fumous aud feeble an enemy. If my grounds be found true, it is all I looke for; but if they cary the force of perſwaſion with them, it is all I can wiſh, and more then I can expect. My onely care is, that you, my deare Countrey-men, may rightly conceiue euen by this ſmalleſt trifle, of the ſinceritie of my meaning in greater matters, neuer to ſpare any paine, that may tend to the procuring of your weale and proſperitie.

A
COUNTERBLASTE TO
Tobacco.

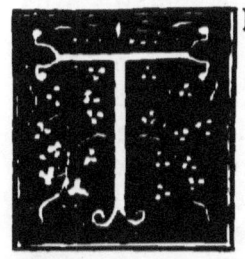

Hat the manifolde abufes of this vile cuftome of *Tobacco* taking, may the better be efpied, it is fit, that firft you enter into confideration both of the firft originall thereof, and likewife of the reafons of the firft entry thereof into this Countrey. For certainely as fuch cuftomes, that haue their firft inftitution either from a godly, neceffary, or honorable ground, and are firft brought in, by the meanes of fome worthy, vertuous, and great Perfonage, are euer, and moft iuftly, holden in great and reuerent eftimation and account, by all wife, vertuous, and temperate fpirits: So fhould it by the contrary, iuftly bring a great difgrace in to that fort of cuftomes, which hauing their originall from bafe corruption and barbarity, doe in like fort, make their firft entry into a Countrey, by an inconfiderate and childifh affectation of Noueltie, as is the true cafe of the firft inuention of *Tobacco* taking, and of the firft entry thereof among vs. For *Tobacco* being a common herbe, which (though vnder diuers names) growes

almoſt euery where, was firſt found out by ſome of the
barbarous *Indians*, to be a Preſeruatiue, or Antidot
againſt the Pockes, a filthy diſeaſe, whereunto theſe
barbarous people are (as all men know) very much
ſubiect, what through the vncleanly and aduſt conſtitution of their bodies, and what through the intemperate
heate of their Climat : ſo that as from them was firſt
brought into Chriſtendome, that moſt deteſtable diſeaſe, ſo from them likewiſe was brought this vſe of
Tobacco, as a ſtinking and vnſauorie Antidot, for ſo
corrupted and execrable a Maladie, the ſtinking Suf-
fumigation whereof they yet vſe againſt that diſeaſe,
making ſo one canker or venime to eate out another.

And now good Countrey men let vs (I pray you)
conſider, what honour or policie can mooue vs to imitate the barbarous and beaſtly maners of the wilde,
godleſſe, and ſlauiſh *Indians*, eſpecially in ſo vile and
ſtinking a cuſtome?   Shall wee that diſdaine to imitate
the maners of our neighbour *France* (hauing the ſtile
of the firſt Chriſtian Kingdom) and that cannot endure
the ſpirit of the Spaniards (their King being now com-
parable in largenes of Dominions, to the great Empe-
ror of *Turkie*)   Shall wee, I ſay, that haue bene ſo long
ciuill and wealthy in Peace, famous and inuincible in
Warre, fortunate in both, we that haue bene euer able
to aide any of our neighbours (but neuer deafed any
of their eares with any of our ſupplications for aſſiſt-
ance) ſhall we, I ſay, without bluſhing, abaſe our ſelues
ſo farre, as to imitate theſe beaſtly *Indians*, ſlaues to
the *Spaniards*, refuſe to the world, and as yet aliens
from the holy Couenant of God?   Why doe we not
as well imitate them in walking naked as they doe? in
preferring glaſſes, feathers, and ſuch toyes, to golde
and precious ſtones, as they doe? yea why do we not
denie God and adore the Deuill, as they doe?

Now to the corrupted baſeneſſe of the firſt vſe of
this *Tobacco*, doeth very well agree the fooliſh and
groundleſſe firſt entry thereof into this Kingdome.   It
is not ſo long ſince the firſt entry of this abuſe amongſt
vs here, as this preſent age cannot yet very well re-

member, both the firſt Author, and the forme of the firſt introduction of it amongſt vs. It was neither brought in by King, great Conquerour, nor learned Doctor of Phiſicke.

With the report of a great diſcouery for a Conqueſt, ſome two or three Sauage men, were brought in, together with this Sauage cuſtome. But the pitie is, the poore wilde barbarous men died, but that vile barbarous cuſtome is yet aliue, yea in freſh vigor: ſo as it ſeemes a miracle to me, how a cuſtome ſpringing from ſo vile a ground, and brought in by a father ſo generally hated, ſhould be welcomed vpon ſo ſlender a warrant. For if they that firſt put it in practiſe heere, had remembred for what reſpect it was vſed by them from whence it came, I am ſure they would haue bene loath, to haue taken ſo farre the imputation of that diſeaſe vpon them as they did, by vſing the cure thereof. For *Sanis non eſt opus medico*, and counter-poiſons are neuer vſed, but where poyſon is thought to precede.

But ſince it is true, that diuers cuſtomes ſlightly grounded, and with no better warrant entred in a Commonwealth, may yet in the vſe of them thereafter, prooue both neceſſary and profitable; it is therefore next to be examined, if there be not a full Sympathie and true Proportion, betweene the baſe ground and fooliſh entrie, and the loathſome, and hurtfull vſe of this ſtinking Antidote.

I am now therefore heartily to pray you to conſider, firſt vpon what falſe and erroneous grounds you haue firſt built the generall good liking thereof; and next, what ſinnes towards God, and fooliſh vanities before the world you commit, in the deteſtable vſe of it.

As for theſe deceitfull grounds, that haue ſpecially mooued you to take a good and great conceit thereof, I ſhall content my ſelfe to examine here onely foure of the principals of them; two founded vpon the Theo-ricke of a deceiuable apparance of Reaſon, and two of them vpon the miſtaken Practicke of generall Experience.

Firſt, it is thought by you a ſure Aphoriſme in the Phyſickes, That the braines of all men, beeing naturally colde and wet, all dry and hote things ſhould be good for them ; of which nature this ſtinking ſuffumigation is, and therefore of good vſe to them.   Of this Argument, both the Propoſition and Aſſumption are falſe, and ſo the Concluſion cannot but be voyd of it ſelfe.   For as to the Propoſition, That becauſe the braines are colde and moiſt, therefore things that are hote and drie are beſt for them, it is an inept conſequence : For man beeing compounded of the foure Complexions, (whoſe fathers are the foure Elements) although there be a mixture of them all in all the parts of his body, yet muſt the diuers parts of our *Microcoſme* or little world within our ſelues, be diuerſly more inclined, ſome to one, ſome to another complexion, according to the diuerſitie of their vſes, that of theſe diſcords a perfeſt harmonie may bee made vp for the maintenance of the whole body.

The application then of a thing of a contrary nature, to any of theſe parts, is to interrupt them of their due funſtion, and by conſequence hurtfull to the health of the whole body.   As if a man, becauſe the Liuer is hote (as the fountaine of blood) and as it were an ouen to the ſtomacke, would therfore apply and weare cloſe vpon his Liuer and ſtomacke a cake of lead ; he might within a very ſhort time (I hope) be ſuſteined very good cheape at an Ordinarie, beſide the cleering of his conſcience from that deadly ſinne of gluttonie.   And as if, becauſe the Heart is full of vitall ſpirits, and in perpetuall motion, a man would therefore lay a heauy pound ſtone on his breaſt, for ſtaying and holding downe that wanton palpitation, I doubt not but his breaſt would bee more bruiſed with the weight thereof, then the heart would be comforted with ſuch a diſagreeable and contrarious cure.   And euen ſo is it with the Braines.   For if a man, becauſe the Braines are colde and humide, would therefore vſe inwardly by ſmells, or outwardly by application, things of hot and drie qualitie, all the gaine that he could make thereof, would onely be to put himſelfe in a great forwardneſſe for running mad, by ouer-watching himſelfe, the coldneſſe and moiſtneſſe of our braine beeing the onely ordinarie meanes that procure our ſleepe and reſt. Indeed I do not denie, but when it falls out that any of theſe, or any part of our bodie growes to be diſtempered, and to tend to an extremitie, beyond the compaſſe of Natures temperate mixture, that in that caſe cures of contrary qualities, to the intemperate inclination of that part, being wiſely prepared and diſcreetely miniſtered, may be both neceſſarie and helpefull for ſtrengthning and aſſiſting Nature in the expulſion of her enemies : for this is the true definition of all profitable Phyſicke.

But firſt theſe Cures ought not to bee vſed, but where there is neede of them, the contrarie whereof, is daily practiſed in this generall vſe of *Tobacco* by all ſorts and complexions of people.

And next, I deny the Minor of this argument, as I haue already ſaid, in regard that this *Tobacco*, is not ſimply of a dry and hot qualitie; but rather hath a certaine venemous facultie ioyned with the heate thereof, which makes it haue an Antipathie againſt nature, as by the hatefull ſmell thereof doeth well appeare. For the Noſe being the proper Organ and conuoy of the ſenſe of ſmelling to the braines, which are the onely fountaine of that ſenſe, doeth euer ſerue vs for an infallible wit-neſſe, whether that Odour which we ſmell, be health-full or hurtfull to the braine (except when it fals out that the ſenſe it ſelfe is corrupted and abuſed through ſome infirmitie, and diſtemper in the braine.) And that the ſuffumigation thereof cannot haue a drying qualitie, it needes no further probation, then that it is a ſmoake, all ſmoake and vapour, being of it ſelfe humide, as drawing neere to the nature of the ayre, and eaſie to be reſolued againe into water, whereof there needes no other proofe but the Meteors, which being bred of nothing elſe but of the vapours and exhalations ſucked vp by the Sunne out of the earth, the Sea, and waters yet are the ſame ſmoakie vapours turned, and transformed into Raynes. Snowes, Deawes, hoare Froſtes, and ſuch like waterie Meteors, as by the contrarie the raynie cloudes are often transformed and euaporated in bluſtering winds.

The ſecond Argument grounded on a ſhow of reaſon is, That this filthie ſmoake, aſwell through the heat and ſtrength thereof, as by a naturall force and qualitie, is able and fit to purge both the head and ſtomacke of Rhewmes and diſtillations, as experience teacheth, by the ſpitting and auoyding fleame, immeadiately after the taking of it.   But the fallacie of this Argument may eaſily appeare, by my late preceding deſcription of the Meteors.   For euen as the ſmoakie vapours ſucked vp by the Sunne, and ſtaied in the loweſt and colde Region of the ayre, are there contraſted into cloudes and turned into raine and ſuch other watery Meteors: So this ſtinking ſmoake being ſucked vp by the Noſe, and impriſoned in the colde and moyſt braines, is by their colde and wett facultie, turned and caſt foorth againe in waterie diſtillations, and ſo are you made free and purged of nothing, but that wherewith you wilfully burdened your ſelues : and therefore are you no wiſer in taking *Tobacco* for purging you of diſtillations, then if for preuenting the Cholike you would take all kinde of windie meates and drinkes. and for preuenting of the Stone, you would take all kinde of meates and drinkes that would breede grauell in the Kidneyes, and then when you were forced to auoyde much winde out of your ſtomacke, and much grauell in your Vrine, that you ſhould attribute the thanke thereof to ſuch nouriſhments as bred thoſe within you, that behoued either to be expelled by the force of Nature, or you to haue *burſt at the broad ſide*, as the Prouerbe is.

As for the other two reaſons founded vpon experience, the firſt of which is, That the whole people would not haue taken ſo generall a good liking there-

of, if they had not by experience found it verie
foueraigne and good for them : For anſwere thereunto
how eaſily the mindes of any people, wherewith God
hath repleniſhed this world, may be drawen to the
fooliſh affectation of any noueltie, I leaue it to the
diſcreet iudgement of any man that is reaſonable.

Doe we not dayly ſee, that a man can no ſooner
bring ouer from beyond the Seas any new forme of
apparell, but that hee can not bee thought a man of
ſpirit, that would not preſently imitate the ſame?
And ſo from hand to hand it ſpreades, till it be practiſed by all, not for any commoditie that is in it, but
only becauſe it is come to be the faſhion. For ſuch is
the force of that naturall Selfe-loue in euery one of vs,
and ſuch is the corruption of enuie bred in the breſt
of euery one, as we cannot be content vnleſſe we imitate euery thing that our fellowes doe, and ſo prooue
our ſelues capable of euery thing whereof they are capable, like Apes, counterfeiting the maners of others, to
our owne deſtruction. For let one or two of the
greateſt Maſters of Mathematickes in any of the two
famous Vniuerſities, but conſtantly affirme any cleare
day, that they ſee ſome ſtrange apparition in the
ſkies : they will I warrant you be ſeconded by the
greateſt part of the Students in that profeſſion : So
loath will they be, to bee thought inferiour to their
fellowes, either in depth of knowledge or ſharpneſſe of
ſight : And therefore the generall good liking and
imbracing of this fooliſh cuſtome, doeth but onely
proceede from that affectation of noueltie, and popular errour, whereof I haue already ſpoken.

The other argument drawen from a miſtaken experience, is but the more particular probation of this
generall, becauſe it is alleaged to be found true by
proofe, that by the taking of *Tobacco* diuers and very
many doe finde themſelues cured of diuers diſeafes
as on the other part, no man euer receiued harme
thereby. In this argument there is firſt a great miſtaking and next a monſtrous abſurditie. For is it not
a very great miſtaking, to take *Non cauſam pro cauſa,*

as they ſay in the Logicks? becauſe peraduenture
when a ſicke man hath had his diſeaſe at the height,
hee hath at that inſtant taken *Tobacco*, and afterward
his diſeaſe taking the naturall courſe of declining, and
conſequently the patient of recouering his health, O
then the *Tobacco* forſooth, was the worker of that
miracle. Beſide that, it is a thing well knowen to all Phiſicians, that the apprehenſion and conceit of the patient
hath by wakening and vniting the vitall ſpirits, and ſo
ſtrengthening nature, a great power and vertue, to cure
diuers diſeaſes For an euident proofe of miſtaking in
the like caſe, I pray you what fooliſh boy, what ſillie
wench, what olde doting wife, or ignorant countrey
clowne, is not a Phiſician for the toothach, for the
cholicke, and diuers ſuch common diſeaſes? Yea,
will not euery man you meete withal, teach you a
ſundry cure for the ſame, and ſweare by that meane
either himſelfe, or ſome of his neereſt kinſmen and
friends was cured? And yet I hope no man is ſo
fooliſh as to beleeue them. And all theſe toyes do
only proceed from the miſtaking *Non cauſam pro
cauſa*, as I haue already ſayd, and ſo if a man chance
to recouer one of any diſeaſe, after he hath taken
Tobacco, that muſt haue the thankes of all. But by
the contrary, if a man ſmoke himſelfe to death with it
(and many haue done) O then ſome other diſeaſe
muſt beare the blame for that fault. So doe olde
harlots thanke their harlotrie for their many yeeres,
that cuſtome being healthfull (ſay they) *ad purgandos
Renes*, but neuer haue minde how many die of the
Pockes in the flower of their youth. And ſo doe olde
drunkards thinke they prolong their dayes, by their
ſwinelike diet, but neuer remember howe many die
drowned in drinke before they be halfe olde.
    And what greater abſurditie can there bee, then to
ſay that one cure ſhall ſerue for diuers, nay, contrarious ſortes of diſeaſes? It is an vndoubted ground
among all Phiſicians, that there is almoſt no ſort either
of nouriſhment or medicine, that hath not ſome thing
in it diſagreeable to ſome part of mans bodie, be-

cauſe, as I haue already ſayd, the nature of the temperature of euery part, is ſo different from another, that
according to the olde prouerbe, That which is good
for the head, is euill for the necke and the ſhoulders.
For euen as a ſtrong enemie, that inuades a towne or
fortreſſe, although in his ſiege thereof, he do belaie
and compaſſe it round about, yet he makes his breach
and entrie, at ſome one or few ſpecial parts thereof,
which hee nath tried and found to bee weakeſt and
leaſt able to refiſt ; ſo ſickeneſſe doth make her particular aſſault, vpon ſuch part or parts of our bodie, as
are weakeſt and eaſieſt to be ouercome by that ſort of
diſeaſe, which then doth aſſaile vs, although all the reſt
of the body by Sympathie feele it ſelfe, to be as it
were belaied, and beſieged by the affliction of that
ſpeciall part, the griefe and ſmart thereof being by the
ſence of feeling diſperſed through all the reſt of our
members.   And therefore the ſkilfull Phiſician preſſes
by ſuch cures, to purge and ſtrengthen that part
which is afflicted, as are only fit for that ſort of diſeaſe,
and doe beſt agree with the nature of that infirme
part ; which being abuſed to a diſeaſe of another nature, would prooue as hurtfull for the one, as helpfull
for the other.   Yea, not only will a ſkilfull and warie
Phiſician bee carefull to vſe no cure but that which is
fit for that ſort of diſeaſe, but he wil alſo conſider all
other circumſtances, and make the remedies ſutable
thereunto : as the temperature of the clime where the
Patient is, the conſtitution of the Planets, the time of
the Moone, the ſeaſon of the yere, the age and complexion of the Patient, and the preſent ſtate of his body,
in ſtrength or weakeneſſe.   For one cure muſt not euer
be vſed for the ſelf-ſame diſeaſe, but according to the
varying of any of the foreſaid circumſtances, that ſort
of remedie muſt be vſed which is fitteſt for the ſame.
Whear by the contrarie in th is caſe, ſuch is the miraculous omnipotencie of our ſtrong taſted *Tobacco*, as
it cures all ſorts of diſeaſes (which neuer any drugge
could do before) in all perſons, and at all times.   It

cures all maner of diſtillations, either in the head or
ſtomacke (if you beleeue their Axiomes) although in
very deede it doe both corrupt the braine, and by
cauſing ouer quicke diſgeſtion, fill the ſtomacke full of
crudities. It cures the Gowt in the feet, and (which
is miraculous) in that very inſtant when the ſmoke
thereof, as light, flies vp into the head, the vertue
thereof, as heauie, runs downe to the little toe. It
helpes all ſorts of Agues. It makes a man ſober that
was drunke. It refreſhes a weary man, and yet makes
a man hungry. Being taken when they goe to bed, it
makes one ſleepe foundly, and yet being taken when a
man is ſleepie and drowſie, it will, as they ſay, awake
his braine, and quicken his vnderſtanding. As for
curing of the Pockes, it ſerues for that vſe but among
the pockie Indian ſlaues. Here in *England* it is refined, and will not deigne to cure heere any other then
cleanly and gentlemanly diſeaſes. O omnipotent power of *Tobacco*! And if it could by the ſmoke thereof
chace out deuils, as the ſmoke of *Tobias* fiſh did (which
I am ſure could ſmel no ſtronglier) it would ſerue for
a precious Relicke, both for the ſuperſtitious Prieſts,
and the inſolent Puritanes, to caſt out deuils withall.

Admitting then, and not confeſſing that the vſe
thereof were healthfull for ſome ſortes of diſeaſes;
ſhould it be vſed for all ſickneſſes? ſhould it be vſed
by all men? ſhould it be vſed at al times? yea ſhould
it be vſed by able, yong, ſtrong, healthful men? Medicine hath that vertue, that it neuer leaueth a man in
that ſtate wherin it findeth him: it makes a ſicke
man whole, but a whole man ſicke. And as Medicine
helpes nature being taken at times of neceſſitie, ſo being euer and continually vſed, it doth but weaken,
wearie, and weare nature. What ſpeake I of Medicine? Nay let a man euery houre of the day, or as oft
as many in this countrey vſe to take *Tobacco*, let a man
I ſay, but take as oft the beſt ſorts of nouriſhments in
meate and drinke that can bee deuiſed, hee ſhall with
the continuall vſe thereof weaken both his head and his

ftomacke : all his members fhall become feeble, his
fpirits dull, and in the end, as a drowfie lazie belly-
god, he fhall euanifh in a Lethargie.

And from this weakneffe it proceeds, that many in
this kingdome hau? had fuch a continuall vfe of taking
this vnfauorie fmoke, as now they are not able to forbeare the fame, no more then an olde drunkard can
abide to be long fober, without falling into an vncur-
able weakeneffe and euill conftitution : for their continuall cuftome hath made to them, *habitum, alteram
naturam* : fo to thofe that from their birth haue bene
continually nourifhed vpon poifon and things venemous, wholefome meates are onely poifonable.

Thus hauing, as I trufte, fufficiently anfwered the
moft principall arguments that are vfed in defence of
this vile cuftome, it refts onely to informe you what
finnes and vanities you commit in the filthie abufe
thereof. Firft, are you not guiltie of finnefull and
fhamefull luft ? (for luft may bee as well in any of the
fenfes as in feeling) that although you bee troubled
with no difeafe, but in perfect health, yet can you
neither be merry at an Ordinarie, nor lafciuious in the
Stewes, if you lacke *Tobacco* to prouoke your appetite
to any of thofe forts of recreation, lufting after it as the
children of Ifrael did in the wilderneffe after Quailes?
Secondly it is, as you vfe or rather abufe it, a branche
of the finne of drunkenneffe, which is the roote of all
finnes : for as the onely delight that drunkards take
in Wine is in the ftrength of the tafte, and the force of
the fume thereof that mounts vp to the braine : for no
drunkards loue any weake, or fweete drinke : fo are
not thofe (I meane the ftrong heate and the fume) the
onely qualities that make *Tobacco* fo delectable to all
the louers of it ? And as no man likes ftrong headie
drinke the firft day (becaufe *nemo repente fit turpiffi-
mus*) but by cuftome is piece and piece allured, while
in the ende, a drunkard will haue as great a thirft to
bee drunke, as a fober man to quench his thirft with
a draught when hee hath need of it : So is not this the
very cafe of all the great takers of *Tobacco*? which

therefore they themfelues do attribute to a bewitching qualitie in it.   Thirdly, is it not the greateft finne of all, that you the people of all fortes of this Kingdome, who are created and ordeined by God to beftowe both your perfons and goods for the maintenance both of the honour and fafetie of your King and Common-wealth, fhould difable your felues in both?   In your perfons hauing by this continuall vile cuftome brought your felues to this fhameful imbecilitie, that you are not able to ride or walke the iourney of a Iewes Sab-both, but you muft haue a reekie cole brought you from the next poore houfe to kindle your *Tobacco* with? whereas he cannot be thought able for any fer-uice in the warres, that cannot endure oftentimes the want of meate, drinke and fleepe, much more then muft hee endure the want of *Tobacco*.   In the times of the many glorious and victorious battailes fought by this Nation, there was no word of *Tobacco*.   But now if it were time of warres, and that you were to make fome fudden *Caualcado* vpon your enemies, if any of you fhould feeke leifure to ftay behinde his fellowe for taking of *Tobacco*, for my part I fhould neuer bee forie for any euill chance that might befall him.   To take a cuftome in any thing that cannot bee left againe, is moft harmefull to the people of any land.   *Mollicies* and delicacie were the wracke and ouerthrow, firft of the Perfian, and next of the Romane Empire.   And this very cuftome of taking *Tobacco* (whereof our pre-fent purpofe is) is euen at this day accounted fo effe-minate among the Indians themfelues, as in the market they will offer no price for a flaue to be fold, whome they finde to be a great *Tobacco* taker.

Now how you are by this cuftome difabled in your goods, let the Gentry of this land beare witneffe, fome of them beftowing three, fome foure hundred pounds a yeere vpon this precious ftinke, which I am fure might be beftowed vpon many farre better vfes.   I read indeede of a knauifh Courtier, who for abufing the fauour of the Emperour *Alexander Seuerus* his Mafter by taking bribes to intercede, for fundry per-

ſons in his Maſters eare, (for whom he neuer once
ɔpened his mouth) was iuſtly choked with ſmoke, with
this doome, *Fumo pereat, qui fumum vendidit :* but of
ſo many ſmoke-buyers, as are at this preſent in this
kingdome, I neuer read nor heard.

And for the vanities committed in this filthie cuſtome, is it not both great vanitie and vncleaneneſſe,
that at the table, a place of reſpeꝗt, of cleanlineſſe, of
modeſtie, men ſhould not be aſhamed, to ſit toſſing of
Tobacco pipes, and puffing of the ſmoke of *Tobacco* one
to another, making the filthy ſmoke and ſtinke thereof,
to exhale athwart the diſhes, and infect the aire, when
very often, men that abhorre it are at their repaſt?
Surely Smoke becomes a kitchin far better then a
Dining chamber, and yet it makes a kitchin alſo oftentimes in the inward parts of men, ſoiling and infeꝗting
them, with an vnꝗuous and oily kinde of Soote, as
hath bene found in ſome great *Tobacco* takers, that
after their death were opened. And not onely meate
time, but no other time nor aꝗtion is exempted from
the publike vſe of this vnciuill tricke : ſo as if the wiues
of *Diepe* liſt to conteſt with this Nation for good maners
their worſt maners would in all reaſon be found at leaſt
not ſo diſhoneſt (as ours are) in this point. The publike
vſe whereof, at all times, and in all places, hath now
ſo farre preuailed, as diuers men very found both in
iudgement, and complexion, haue bene at laſt forced
to take it alſo without deſire, partly becauſe they were
aſhamed to ſeeme ſingular, (like the two Philoſophers
that were forced to duck themſelues in that raine
water, and ſo become fooles aſwell as the reſt of the
people) and partly, to be as one that was content to
eate Garlicke (which hee did not loue) that he might
not be troubled with the ſmell of it, in the breath of
his fellowes. And is it not a great vanitie, that a man
cannot heartily welcome his friend now, but ſtraight
they muſt bee in hand with *Tobacco*? No it is become
in place of a cure, a point of good fellowſhip, and
he that will refuſe to take a pipe of *Tobacco* among
his fellowes, (though by his own eleꝗtion he would

rather feele the fauour of a Sinke) is accounted peeuiſh
and no good company, euen as they doe with tippeling
in the cold Eaſterne Countries.   Yea the Miſtreſſe
cannot in a more manerly kinde, entertaine her ſer-
uant, then by giuing him out of her faire hand a pipe
of *Tobacco*.   But herein is not onely a great vanitie,
but a great contempt of Gods good giftes, that the
ſweeteneſſe of mans breath, being a good gift of God,
ſhould be willfully corrupted by this ſtinking ſmoke,
wherein I muſt confeſſe, it hath too ſtrong a vertue :
and ſo that which is an ornament of nature, and can
neither by any artifice be at the firſt acquired, nor
once loſt, be recouered againe, ſhall be filthily corrupted with an incurable ſtinke, which vile qualitie is
as directly contrary to that wrong opinion which is
holden of the wholeſomneſſe thereof, as the venime of
putrifaction is contrary to the vertue Preſeruatiue.

Moreouer, which is a great iniquitie, and againſt all
humanitie, the husband ſhall not bee aſhamed, to
reduce thereby his delicate, wholeſome, and cleane
complexioned wife, to that extremitie, that either ſhee
muſt alſo corrupt her ſweete breath therewith, or elſe
reſolue to liue in a perpetuall ſtinking torment.

Haue you not reaſon then to bee aſhamed, and to
forbeare this filthie noueltie, ſo baſely grounded, ſo
fooliſhly receiued and ſo groſſely miſtaken in the right
vſe thereof?   In your abuſe thereof ſinning againſt
God, harming your ſelues both in perſons and goods,
and raking alſo thereby the markes and notes of vanitie
vpon you : by the cuſtome thereof making your ſelues
to be wondered at by all forraine ciuil Nations, and
by all ſtrangers that come among you, to be ſcorned
and contemned.   A cuſtome lothſome to the eye, hatefull to the Noſe, harmefull to the braine, dangerous to
the Lungs, and in the blacke ſtinking fume thereof, neereſt reſembling the horrible Sti-
gian ſmoke of the pit that is
bottomeleſſe.

The foregoing Invective was written by the King of Great Britain. How early its royal authorſhip was avowed, I know not : but it was generally known long before its inſertion in the collected edition of the King's *Workes*, publiſhed in 1616.

But King James ſtopped not, in his Cruſade againſt Tobacco, at words. In the following *Commiſſio pro Tabacco* he added Fines and Blows.

JAMES, by the grace of God *&c.* to our right Trustie and right Welbeloued Cousen and Counsellor, *Thomas Earle of Dorset* our High Treasourer of Englande, Greetinge.

Whereas *Tabacco*, being a Drugge of late Yeres found out, and by Merchants, as well Denizens as Strangers, brought from forreign Partes in small quantitie into this Realm of England and other our Dominions, was used and taken by the better sort both then and nowe onelye as Phisicke to preserve Healthe, and is now at this Day, through evell Custome and the Tolleration thereof, excessivelie taken by a nomber of ryotous and disordered Persons of meane and base Condition, whoe, contrarie to the use which Persons of good Callinge and Qualitye make thereof, doe spend most of there tyme in that idle Vanitie, to the evill example and corrupting of others, and also do consume that Wages whiche manye of them gett by theire Labour, and wherewith there Families should be releived, not caring at what Price they buye that Drugge, but rather devisinge how to add to it other Mixture, therebye to make it the more delightfull to their Taste, though so much the more costly to there Purse ; by which great and imoderate takinge of *Tabacco* the Health of a great nomber of our People is impayred, and theire Bodies weakened and made unfit for Labor, the Estates of many mean Persons soe decayed and consumed as they are thereby dryven to unthrifüe Shifts onelie to maynteyne their gluttonous exercise thereof, besides that also a great part of the Treasure of our Lande is spent and exhausted by this onely Drugge so licentiously abused by the meaner sorte, all which enormous Inconveniences ensuinge thereuppon We doe well perceave to proceed principally from the great quantitie of *Tabacco* daily brought into this our Realm of England and Dominions of Wales from the Partes beyond the Seas by Merchauntes and others, which Excesse We conceave might in great part be restrayned by some good Imposition to be laid uppon it, whereby it is likelie that a lesse Quantitie of *Tabacco* will hereafter be broughte into this our Realm of England, Dominion of Wales and Town of Barwick then in former tymes, and yet sufficient store to serve for their necessarie use who are of the better sort, and have and will use the same with Moderation to preserve their Healthe ;

We do therefore will and command you our Treasurer of Englande, and herebye also warrant and aucthorise you to geve order to all Customers Comptrollers Searchers Surveyors, and other Officers of our Portes, that, from and after the sixe and twentith Day of October next comynge, they shall demaunde and take to our use of all Merchauntes, as well Englishe as Strangers, and of all others whoe shall bringe in anye *Tabacco* into this Realme, within any Potte Haven or Creek belonging to any theire severall Charges, the Somme of *Six Shillinges and eighte Pence* uppon everye Pound Waight thereof, over and above the Custome of *Twoo Pence* uppon the Pounde Waighte usuallye paide heretofore ;

And for the better execution hereof, bothe in the Reformation of the saide Abuses, and for the avoydinge of all Fraude and Deceipte concerninge the Paymente of the saide Imposition and Custome, Our Will and Pleasure is that you shall in our Name straightlye charge and commaunde all Collectors Customers Comptrollers Surveyors, and other Officers whatsoever to whome the same maye belonge, that they suffer noe Entries to be made of anye Tabacco at anye tyme hereafter to be broughte into anye Porte Haven or Creeke within this our Realme of Englande, and Dominion of Wales, and

H

Towne of Barwicke, or anye parte of the same, by anye Englishe or Stranger, or anye other Persone whatsoever, befőre the saide Custome and Imposition before specified be firste satisfied and paide, or Composition made for the same with our saide Customers, Collectors, or other Officers to whome the enme apperteyneth, uppon Payne that if anye Merchaunte Englishe or Straunger, or other whatsoever, shall presume to bringe in anye of the saide *Tabacco*, before suche Payemente and Satisfactione firste made, That then he shall not onelie forfeite the saide *Tabacco*, but alsoe shall undergoe suche furthere Penalties and corporall Punishmente as the Qualitie of suche soe highe a Contempte against our Royall and expresse Commaundemente in this mannere published shall deserve.

Wytnes our self at *Westminster* the seaventeenth Day of October. [1604].

Per ipsum Regem.

Rymer *Fœdera*, xvi. 601. Ed. 1715.

Sir ROBERT AYTON [b. 1570—d. an unmarried man in 1638] left among his MSS. the following Sonnet, firſt printed among his *Poems*, Edinburgh, 1844. Ed. by C. Roger.

ON TOBACCO.

Forsaken of all comforts but these two,
My faggot and my pipe, I sit and muse
On all my crosses, and almost accuse
The Heav'ns for dealing with me as they do.
Then Hope steps in, and with a smiling brow
Such cheerful expectations doth infuse
As makes me think ere long I cannot choose
But be some grandee, whatsoe'er I'm now.
But having spent my pipe, I then perceive
That hopes and dreams are cousins—both deceive.
Then mark I this conclusion in my mind,
It's all one thing—both tend into one scope—
To live upon Tobacco and on Hope,
The one's but smoke, the other is but wind. *p.* 53.

1606. "The copy of a Letter written by E. D. Doctour of Phyficke to a Gentleman, by whom it was publifhed. The former part conteineth *Rules for the preferuation of health, and preuenting of all difeafes vntil extreme olde age.* Herein is inferted *the Authours opinion of Tabacco.*" . . .

E. D. argues that Tabacco is 1) not safe for youth : 2) it shorteneth life : (3 it breedeth many diseases : (4) it breedeth melancholy : 5 it hurteth the minde : 6 it is ill for the Smokers' issue : 7, it shorteneth life : and

"To conclude, sith it is so hurtfull and dangerous to youth. I wish (in compassion of them that it might haue the pernitious nature expressed in the name, and that it were as well knowen by the name of Youths-bane, as by the name of Tabacco." *pp.* 3-5.

1607. *A fixe-folde Politician*, by J[OHN] M[ELTON], has the following allufion to Tobacco Smoking :—

And as the enterludes may be tearmed, the Schoole-houses of vanitie, and wantonnes ; so these [vaine poets and plaiers] are the schoolemaisters thereof : and methinks they who haue tasted of the sweete fountaine water, running from their Academick mothers breasts, by this, if nothing else shold be deterred from their scribling profeffion, that they see their writings and conceits sold at a common doore to euery base companion for a penny. But most of their conceits are too deere at that rate, and therefore may well bee had in the same request that Tobacco is now, which was wont to be taken of great gentlemen, and gallants, now made a frequent and familiar Companion of euery Tapster and Horse-keeper. And their conceits are likest Tobacco of any thing : for as that is quickly kindled, *Conceits sauo-* makes a stinking smoake, and quickly goes out, but leaues *ring of no* and inhering stinke in the nostrils and stomackes of the *iudgement or* takers, not to be drawne out, but by putting in a worse sa- *studdie like* uour, as of Onions and Garlick, (according to the prouerbe : *Tobacco* the smel of Garlicke takes away the stink of dunghils,) so *smoke.* the writing of ordinarye Play-bookes, Pamphlets, and such like, may be tearmed the mushrum conceptions of idle braines, moste of them are begotte ouer night in Tobacco smoake and muld-sacke, and vttered and deliuered to the worlds presse by the helpe and midwifery of a caudle the next morning. *pp.* 34-36.

   1610. (1.) 'E[DMUND] G[ARDINER]. Gent. and Practitioner in Physicke,' wrote a medical defence, under the title of *The Triall of Tabacco. Wherein, his worth is most worthily expressed, as, in the name, nature, and qualitie of the sayd hearb, his speciall vse in all Physicke, with the true and right vse of taking it,* &c. . . .

   (2.) Under this year may also be put—GEORGE SANDYS. *A Relation of a Journey begun An. Dom.* 1610. *Foure Bookes. Containing a description of the Turkish Empire, of Ægypt, of the Holy Land, of the Remote parts of Italy, and Islands adioyning.* London. 1615.

   The *Turkes* are also incredible takers of *Opium,* whereof the lesser *Asia* affordeth them plenty : carrying it about them both in peace and in warre ; which they say expelleth all feare, and makes them couragious : but I rather thinke giddy headed, and turbulent dreamers ; by them, as should seeme by what hath bene said, religiously affected. And perhaps for the selfe same cause they also delight in Tobacco ; they take it through reeds that haue ioyned vnto them great heads of wood to containe it : I doubt not but lately taught them, as brought them by the English : and were it not sometimes lookt into (for *Morat Bassa* not long since commanded a pipe to be thrust through the nose of a *Turke,* and so to be led in derision through the Citie,) no question but it would proue a principall commodity. Neuerthelesse they will take it in corners, and are so ignorant therein, that that which in Eng-land is not saleable, doth passe here amongst them for most excellent. Bk. I. *p.* 66.

So England took Tobacco first to Turkey.

   1611. *Perfuming of Tobacco, and the great Abuse committed in it.* See Lowndes.

   1614. (1.) WILLIAM BARCLAY, M.A., M.D., published at Edinburgh,—what was perhaps the first flat contradiction to the *Counterblaste*—viz.: *Nepenthes, or the Vertues of Tabacco.* This tract—which I should, had space permitted, have been glad to have entirely reprinted here—was published by the Spalding Club in their *Miscellany,* i. *pp.* 257-274. It begins thus—

HERCVLES to obey the commandement and will of IVNO, busied him-selfe to ouerthrow the most famous monsters of his time, his Armes were a bagge and a club. A most worthie Ladie, and, if I durst say so, the very IVNO of our Ile hath commanded me to destroy some monstruous Diseases so that to imitate the most chiualrous Chiftan of the worlde, I haue armed my selfe with a boxe for his bagge, and a pipe for his club : a boxe to conserue my *Tabacco,* and a pipe to vse it, by those two Godwilling, to ouercome many maladies. If the hostes of such Diseases do not betray my endeuoures to their hating and hated guests by not vsing or abusing my weapons. But before I enter in the list, I must whet as it were my wits with these two points, First why doe I treat of a matter so often handled by so many, so odious to Princes, so pernicious to sundrie, and so costly to all?

Secondly why doe I as another CLODIVS reueale *mysteria bonæ Deæ*, and prophane the secrets of Physicke? I answere that a good matter is not the worse to be maintained by many: and *Plus vident oculi quam oculus.* As concerning the hatred of Princes, one mans meate is another mans poyson. The wine prince of liquors hateth vehemently colworts, and yet beere, aile, sider water, oyle, honey, and all other liquors doe well agree with colworts. The king of *France* drinketh neuer *Orleans* wine notwithstanding his subjects doe loue it well.

I know sundrie men that haue such Antipathie with butter that they dare not smell it. It hath bene pernicious to sundrie I grant it, so hath wine, so hath bread, so hath gold, so hath land, and what so wholsome thing is that cannot be turned to abuse? If it be costly vse the lesse of it. What? is not Rheubarbe coastly? is not Muske coastly? is not *Ambergreese* coastly? As touching the second point of my reuealling this secret of Physicke, I answere, I mean but to reforme the harme which proceedeth of the abuse, and to shew to my countrey men that I am more willing to pleasure them then to profite my selfe, neither did I sweare to conceale that point when in a robe of purpure I wedded the metamorphosed DAPHNE. It resteth now to vnfold what moued me to entitule this treatise *Nepenthes,* because it hath certaine mellifluous delicacie, which deliteth the senses, and spirits of man with a mindful obliuion, insomuch that it maketh and induceth κακῶν ἐπίζηθον ἀ πάντων the forgetting of all sorrowes and miseries. And there is such hostilitie betwene it and melancholie, that it is the only medicament in the world ordained by nature to entertaine good companie: insomuch that it worketh neuer so well, as when it is giuen from man to man, as a pledge of friendshippe and amitie.

[The countrey which God hath honoured and blessed with this happie and holy herbe, doth call it in the natiue language *Petum*, the Spaniards, who haue giuen it the right of naturalitie in their soyle, terme it *Tabacco*, the Frenchmen which haue receiued it in their countrey as in a colonie call it *Nicotian*, in this our Ile of *Brittaine*, as in all other maritime parts, we vse the Spanish name of *Tabacco*. But esteeming it worthie of a more loftie name, I haue chosen for gossip the faire and famous *Helena*, and giuen to her the honour to name this most profitable plant, *Nepenthes.*

Albeit this herbe disdaines not to be nourished in many gardens in *Spaine*, in *Italie, France, Flanders, Germanie* and *Brittaine*, yet neuerthelesse only that which is fostered in *India* and brought home by Mariners and Traffiquers is to be vsed, as after you shall heare the reason is.

Non omnis fert omnia tellus.

But auarice and greedines of gaine haue moued the Marchants to apparell some *European* plants with *Indian* coats, and to enstall them in shops as righteous and legittime *Tabacco* . . . . So that the most fine, best, and purest is that which is brought to *Europe* in leaues, and not rolled in puddings, as the English Navigators first brought home. . . .

In *Tabacco* there is nothing which is not medecin, the root, the stalke, the leaues, the seeds, the smoke, the ashes, and to be more particular, *Tabacco* may serue for the vse of man either greene or dry. . . .

To the cure and peregrination of an armie of malad·es, *Tabacco* must be used after this maner. Take of leafe *Tabacco* as much as being folded together, may make a round ball of such bignesse that it may fill the patient's mouth, and inclyne his face downward towards the ground, keeping the mouth open, not mouing a whit with his tongue, except now and then to waken the medicament, there shall flow such a flood of water from his brain and his stomacke, and from all parts of his body that it shall be a wonder. This he must do fasting in the morning, and if it be for preseruation, and the body very cacochyme, or full of euil humours, he must take it once a weeke, otherwise once a month: But if it bee to cure the Epilepsie or Hydropisie once euery day. Thus haue I vsed *Tabacco* my self, and thus vsed *Tabacco, Iean Greis* a venerable old man at *Nantes* in the French Britain, who liued whill he was six score yeares of age, and who was known for the only refuge of the poore afflicted souldiers of *Venus* when they were wounded with the French Pickes, I should haue said Pockes. Thus much for the vse of *Tabacco* in substance. As concerning the smoke, it may be taken more frequently, and for the said effects, but always fasting, and with an emptie stomack, not as the English abuses do, which make a smoke-boxe of their skull, more fit to be caried vnder his arme that selleth at Paris, *dunoir a noircir* to blacke men's shoes, then to carie the braine of him that can not walke, can not ryde except the *Tabacco* Pype be in his mouth. I chanced in company on a tyme with an English merchant in *Normandie* betweene *Rowen* and *New-hauen*. This fellow was a merrie man, but at euery house he must have a *Cole* to kindle his *Tabacco*: the Frenchmen wondered, and I laughed at his intemperancie. But there is one *William Alsop* an honest man dwelling in Bishops-gate street, hard within the gate that selleth the best *Tabacco* in *England*, and vseth it most discreetly. . . .

(2.) " *The Honeſtie of this Age.* Proouing by good circum- ſtance that the world was neuer honeſt till now. By BARNABEE RYCH Gentleman, Seruant to the Kings moſt Excellent Maieſtie." has the following.

But he that some fortie or fifty yeares sithens, should haue asked after a *Pickadilly*, I wonder who could haue vnderstood him, or could haue told what a *Pickadilly* had beene, either fish or flesh.

But amongst the trades that are newly taken vp, this trade of *Tobacco* doth exceede : and the money that is spent in smoake is vnknowne, and (I thinke) vnthought on, and of such a smoake as is more vaine, then the smoake of fayre words, for that (they say) will serue to feede *Fooles*, but this smoake maketh *Fooles* of *Wisemen*: mee thinks experience were enough to teach the most simple witted, that before *Tobacco* was euer knowne in *England*, that we liued in as perfect health, and as free from sicknesse, as we haue done sithens, and looke vppon those (whereof there are a number at this present houre) that did neuer take *Tobacco* in their liues, and if they doe not liue as healthsome in bodie, and as free from all manner of diseases, as those that doe take it fastest : they say it is good for a *Cold*, for a *Pose*, for *Rewms*, for *Aches*, for *Dropsies*, and for all manner of diseases proceeding of moyst humours : but I cannot see but that those that doe take it fastest, are asmuch (or more) subiect to all these infirmities, (yea and to the poxe it selfe) as those that haue nothing at all to doe with it : then what a wonderfull expence might very well bee spared, that is spent and consumed in this needlesse vanitie.

There is not so base a groome, that commes into an *Alehouse* to call for his pot, but he must haue his *pipe* of *Tobacco*, for it is a commoditie that is nowe as vendible in euery *Tauerne, Inne*, and *Ale house*, as eyther Wine, Ale, or Beare, and for *Apothicaries Shops, Grosers Shops, Chaundlers Shops*, they are (almost) neuer without company, that from morning till night are still taking of *Tobacco*, what a number are there besides, that doe keepe houses, set open shoppes, that haue no other trade to liue by, but by the selling of Tobacco.

I haue heard it tolde that now very lately, there hath bin a *Cathalogue* taken of all those new erected houses that haue set vppe that Trade of sell- ing Tobacco, in London and neare about London, and if a man may beleeue what is confidently reported, there are found to be vpward of 7000. houses, that doth liue by that trade.

I cannot say whether they number Apothicaries shoppes, Grosers shops, and Chaundlers shops in this computation, but let it be that these were thrust in to make vppe the number : let vs now looke a little into the *Vidimus* of the matter, and let vs cast vppe but a sleight account, what the expence might be that is consumed in this smoakie vapoure.

If it be true that there be 7000. shops, in and about London, that doth vent Tobacco, as it is credibly reported that there be ouer and aboue that number: it may well bee supposed. to be but an ill customed shoppe, that taketh not fiue shillings a day, one day with another, throughout the whole yeare, or if one doth take lesse, two other may take more : but let vs make our account, but after 2 shillings sixe pence a day, for he that taketh lesse than that, would be ill able to pay his rent, or to keepe open his Shop Windowes, neither would *Tobacco* houses make such a muster as they doe, and that almost in euery Lane, and in euery by-corner round about *London*.

Let vs then reckon thus. 7000. halfe Crowns a day amounteth just to 31,9375 poundes a yeare. *Summa totalis*, All spent in *smoake*.

I doe not reckon now what is spent in Tauernes, in Innes, in Alehouses, nor what gentlemen doe spend in their owne houses and chambers, it would amount to a great reckoning, but if I cou'de deliuer truly what is spent throughout the whole Realme of England, in that idle vanitie, I thinke it woulde make a number of good people (that haue anie feare of God in them) to lament, that such a masse of Treasure, should be so basely consumed, that might be imployed to many better purposes.—*pp*. 25–27.

(3.) JOSHUA SYLVESTER, the tranflator of Du Bartas, wrote a poem, under the title of *Tobacco battered ; and the Pipes fhattered (About their Eares that idlely Idolize fo bafe and barbarous a Weed; or at least-wife ouer-loue fo loathfome Vanitie:) by A Velley of holy Shot thundered from Mount Helicon*.   The calibre of this Invective may be meafured by its concluding lines—

.   .   .   How iuster will the Heau'nly GOD,
Th' *Eternal*, punish with infernal Rod,
In Hell's darke (Fornace, with black *Fumes*, to choak)
Those, that on Earth will still *offend in Smoak!*
Offend their Friends, with a Most *vn-Respect*:
Offend their Wiues and Children, with Neglect:
Offend the Eyes, with foule and loathsom Spawlings:
Offend the Nose, with filthy Fumes exhalings:
Offend the Eares, with lowd lewd *Execrations*:
Offend the Mouth, with ougly Excreations:
Offend the *Sense*, with stupefying *Sense*:
Offend the Weake, to follow their *Offense*:
Offend the Body, and offend the Minde:
Offend the *Conscience* in a fearefull kinde:
Offend their *Baptisme*, and their *Second Birth*:
Offend the *Maiestie* of Heau'n and Earth.
    Woe to the World because of Such *Offenses*:
So voluntaire, so voyd of all pretenses
Of all *Excuse* (saue *Fashion, Custome, Will*)
In so apparant, proued, granted, *Ill*.
Woe, woe to them by Whom *Offences* come,
So scandalous to All our CHRISTENDOME.

1615. *An Advice how to plant Tobacco in England: and how to bring it to colour and perfection, to whom it may be profitable, and to whom harmfull.   The vertues of the Hearbe in generall, as well in the outward application as taken in FVME.   With the danger of the Spanifh Tobacco.*   Written by C. T.

This work gives us a good idea of the rapid growth of Tobacco Smoking in England.

I haue heard it reported, by men of good iudgement, that there is paid out of England and Ireland, neere the value of two hundred thousand pounds euery yeare for Tobacco; and that the greatest part thereof is bought for ready money.   Sure I am, that when our Englifhmen fer these seuen or eight yeares last past, traded for it at *Trinidado*, or in *Orenoque*, that great store of Gold, Siluer, Coine, and plate was carried hence, and giuen to the Spaniard there in exchange.   For so greedy were our Englifh of the Indian Tobacco, as where in the beginning of our traffique there, some yeares since, the Spaniards as in all new plantations' were prest with all sorts of warts; and had neither cloathes to couer them, nor shooes to tread on, nor bread to eate, and did therefore exchange their Tobacco for Fish, Wine, Aqua-vtæ, all sorts of lasting food, for woollen stockins, hats, threed hatchets, and the like: they became in a short time so cloyd with all these commodities, as nothing (some Silkes, and Cloath of Siluer and Gold excepted) but ready Money, and Siluer plate could content them.

This Trade therefore, where the Treasure of this land is vented for smoke, cannot but greatly preiudiçe the Common-weale: which although it were in some sort tollerable, by reason that many shippes and Mariners were employed, and that thereby wee kept our knowledge of the West Indies, and bred many sufficient Marriners : yet seeing the Spaniards haue now vtterly banished our Merchants, and put all to the sword, or to a more cruell death, which they can maister, or betray in those parts : I haue thought good, as well for the keeping within the Land of the Treasure before spoken of, then carried into the Indies, and now into Spaine, as for other respects hereafter remembred; to instruct those of our Nation how to sow, plant and perfect this drugge.

For besides the ill exchange made for this fantasticall merchandize, and besides, the extreame rate, and price of the Indian Tobacco, of which the greatest part is sold for ten times the value of pepper, and the best of it, weight for weight, for the finest siluer; it is hard to find one pound weight in fiue hundred, that is not sophisticate.

The naturall colour of Tobacco is a deepe yellow, or a light tawnie : and when the Indians themselues sold it vs for Kniues, Hatchets, Beads, Belles, and like merchandise, it had no other complexion, as all the Tobacco at this day hath, which is brought from the coast of Guinna, from Saint *Vincents*, from Saint *Lucia*, from *Dominica*, and other places, where we buy it but of the naturall people, and all these sorts are cleane, and so is that of St. *Domingo*, where the Spaniards haue not yet learned the Art of Sophistication.

There is also a sort of Caraccas Tobacco, which the Indians make vp, and sell to the Spaniards, which is wholesome enough; but there comes little of it into England.

Now besides these harmefull mixtures, if our English which delight in Indian Tobacco, had seene how the Spanish slaues make it vp, how they dresse their sores, and pockie vlcers, with the same vnwasht hands with which they slubber and annoynt the Tobacco, and call it sauce *Per los perros Luteranos*, for *Lutheran* dogges, they would not so often draw it into their heads and through their noses as they doe : yea many a filthy sauour should they find therein, did not the smell of the hunny maister it, which smell euery man may plainly perceiue that takes of the blacke roll Tabacco, brought from *Orenoque*, *Trinidado*, and else-where.

1616. JOHN DEACON—who appears to have been another Phillip Stubbes—dedicated *Tobacco tortured ; or the filthie fume of Tobacco refined* : to James I.

This work is in the form of a dialogue between *Capniftus* and *Hydrophorus*. It is divided into two parts : (1.) The Fume of Tobacco taken inward, is very pernicions vnto the Body. (2.) The Fume of Tobacco taken inward, is too too profluuious for many of our *Tobacconists* purfes, and moft pernicious to the publike State.

The following extracts will fhow the nature of the work.

Capn. Alas poore *Tobacco*, my pretie *Tobacco*; thou that haft bene hitherto accompted the Ale-knights armes, the Beere-brewers badge, the Carousers crest, the Drunkards darling, the Draffe-sacks delight, the Easterlings ensigne, the Fantasticals foretresse, the Gormandizers glorie, the hungry Hostesses ale-pole, the Mad-braines merriment, the New-fangles noueltie, the Poope-noddies paramour, the Ruffians reflection, the Swil-boles swine-troffe, the Tinkers trull, the Tospots protection, the Vintners vintage, and the vnthrifts pasport : thou must now (I feare me) bee enforced forthwith to take thy farewell to-wards the vttermost parts of *India*, from whence thou were first transported to *England* by vicious and wild dispositions. . . . . *p.* 57.

Hydr. First therefore for the exceeding high rate that this *Tobacco* hath euer bene at since the very first arriuall thereof into *England*, thou thy selfe, and all our *Tobacconists*, are able to say this of your owne proper knowledge:

namely, that the same hath vsually bene sold by the pound, for twentie
nobles, fiue, foure, or three pounds: yea and when it came to the lowest
price, it could not bee had vnder foure markes or fortie shillings, which
amounteth to three shillings foure pence an ounce at the least.   Is not this
(thinkest thou an exceeding high rate for filthie *Tobacco?* . . . *p.* 61.

Hydr. Concerning therefore that former superfluous and riotous waste, which
those *Tobacconists* do so wilfully make about their beastly *Tobacco fumes*,
do tell me in good sadnesse, whether it be not a superfluous waste, for any
man of great place, to paddle forth yearely one hundred pounds at the least,
for an hundred gallons of filthy fumes? for a Gentleman of meaner condition,
to be at fortie pound annuall expences, about hare fortie pottels of stinking
flames, for a Yeoman, an Husbandman, an Artificer, a Trades-man, a Tinker,
a Shoomaker, or a Cobbler, to bestow weekely some three shillings four-
pence at the least, for but one onely ounce of fantastical fooleries? . . . *p.* 62.

Hydr. So as by these meanes) they make great noble Persons, but single-
soaled Gentlemen; well bred Gentelmen, but bare thredded Yeomen; bounti-
full Yeomen, but beggerly Husbandmen, hospitious Husbandmen, but shifting
Trades-men, artificous Trades-men but conicatching companions, conicatching companions, but vagabond rogues.   Thus thou mayest plainly perceiue
how these their intoxicating *Tobacco fumes* are able in an vnperceiuable and
Circean manner to transforme nobilitie into gentrie, gentrie into yeomanrie,
yeomanrie into husbandry, husbandrie into maunuarie, manuarie into manubiarie, manubiarie into a vagrant and retchlesse roguerie, and what not
besides? *p.* 65.

(2.) The *Counterblaste* was reprinted this year in Bishop
Montagu's edition of James' *Workes.*

1616. Bishop Montagu published a Latin translation of the
King's works : in which the *Counterblaste* appears as *Misocapnus,
seu de Abusu Tabacci.*   This provoked a Polish Jesuit to write
Antimisocapnus, a tract which I have not met with.

We cannot better conclude these scattered notices, than with
the following poem : sometimes called *Tobacco Spiritualized :* but
which is evidently *reprinted* in *Two Broadsides,* &c.   1672 : see
No. 4, *p.* 6.

> The *Indian* Weed withered quite,
> Green at Noon, cut down at Night:
> Shews thy decay, all Flesh is hay:
> Thus think, then drink *Tobacco.*
>
> The Pipe that is so lilly-white,
> Shews Thee to be a mortal Wight,
> And euen such gone with a touch:
> Thus think, then drink *Tobacco.*
>
> And when the Smoke ascends on high,
> Think thou behold'st the Vanity
> Of worldly stuff, gone with a puff:
> Thus think, then drink *Tobacco.*
>
> And when the Pipe grows foul within,
> Think on the Soul defil'd with Sin,
> And then the Fire it doth require:
> Thus think, then drink *Tobacco.*
>
> The Ashes that are left behind
> May serve to put thee still in mind,
> That unto Dust return thou must:
> Thus think, then drink *Tobacco.*

Answered by *George Withers* thus,
> Thus think, drink no *Tobacco.*

www.ingramcontent.com/pod-product-compliance
Lightning Source LLC
Chambersburg PA
CBHW032018010726
47493CB00007B/2465